He Doesn't Deserve My Love:

Renaissance Collection

He Doesn't Deserve My Love:

Renaissance Collection

Ashley Cruse

www.urbanbooks.net

Urban Books, LLC
300 Farmingdale Road, NY-Route 109
Farmingdale, NY 11735

He Doesn't Deserve My Love: Renaissance Collection

ISBN 13: 978-1-62286-610-6
ISBN 10: 1-62286-610-X

First Trade Paperback Printing June 2017
Printed in the United States of America

10 9 8 7 6 5 4 3 2 1

Distributed by Kensington Publishing Corp.
Submit Orders to:
Customer Service
400 Hahn Road
Westminster, MD 21157-4627
Phone: 1-800-733-3000
Fax: 1-800-659-2436

He Doesn't Deserve My Love:

Renaissance Collection

by

Ashley Cruse

This novel is dedicated to Jayson, Jeromiah, Jeaniece, Aubri, Kyair, and Kynzi Cruse.
(my niece, nephews, and my children)

When life throws you guys lemons, take them, squeeze them, and sell the hell out of that lemonade.

Acknowledgments

My gratitude goes to my very supportive family and friends, including my daddy, my grandma, all my aunts and uncles, and my sisters, Shinee, Jessica, Cherish, Emerald, and Jahnay. There are too many of you guys to name, but you all have my heartfelt thanks. It's been quite a journey. Knowledge is very powerful, and I'm so thankful for the support from my Cruse and Kershaw side.

Thank you to Shaunta Kenerly and Yushekia Mason. Shaun, you have no idea how much of a blessing you really and truly are. I am so glad for your brain. Can't wait to introduce the world to Gemini when we get it done. Shekia, my partner in crime, we are going to take this over.

Racquel Williams and the rest of the RWP family, it's such a blessing to be with you guys. You certainly make moves, and you care about your authors as well. Love it.

A big thanks goes to my writing sisters, Cynthia Rubio, Natalie Sade, and Nikki Rountree.

I love you and miss you, Willie T. Kershaw, my grandpa, my bestest friend, and my mom. It's your gifts you blessed me with, so I know you're super proud.

Chapter 1

Dollie

"Can I see your ID, please?" I heard the heavyset guard ask the couple in front of me.

I was at Formby State Jail, a prison that was located four and a half hours away from where I lived in Abilene, Texas. It was about forty-five minutes outside of Lubbock. I had not been trippin' at all about the ride up there. After all, I loved road trips, no matter the conditions or circumstances.

I was standing patiently in line, waiting my turn. I had come to visit my man, right along with several other people who had come to visit their friends or loved ones. Ahead of me was a cute elderly couple. I thought quietly to myself, trying to guess who they were here to see. Was it their son? Maybe their nephew, grandson, father, or brother? Hmm. I would soon find out.

My boyfriend, the one I had come to see, was Corey Knight. He had been locked up for violating his probation. From what he had told me, he was on probation for minor weed cases and a dope charge.

We had gotten together just six months before his probation officer had him arrested. During those six months, I had kind of figured it was bound to happen sooner or later. Corey had been way too wild and hadn't seemed to care too much about his probation regulations. His UA had been dirty three times, and when I'd taken him to go report, he came out in handcuffs.

On the cool, I think he'd known what it was. That was probably why he'd been in the bathroom, snortin' up all that coke and smokin' that blunt with his homies, before we left that day. He'd walked in high as a kite to see his probation officer because that was the last time he would be able to feed his addiction for a while.

He'd understood I didn't like that shit. He had just kept getting fucked up and using, anyway. Corey was cool as fuck when he was sober. It was when his ass got messed up on all those drugs that he became like Dr. Jekyll and Mr. Hyde. A straight-up asshole. I should have left his ass *before* that day he had to report. But since I was his girl, I had had to do my part.

Win, lose, or draw, you never turned your back on somebody when they needed you the most. Therefore, I had chosen to ride it out. Mainly because he needed somebody. Plus, a part of me thought that if he would just sit down and sober up, he would realize he had something good going with me.

He was afraid I wasn't going to hold his ass down. He told me every chance he got that I would leave him high and dry, just like them other hoes. I knew better. Actions always spoke louder than words. Being there for him when he needed somebody the most spoke volumes. At least that was how I felt.

I could have thrown up the deuces and gone on about my business, but to me, he was special. He was something I had never had before. Corey had two different people living inside of him. One of his personalities, I was in love with. The other, I could not stand. The one I loved was a sweetheart. He adored my son, and he cherished me. This Corey was sober, and when all he did was smoke some of that herb, he was still cool. We could have good conversations about anything. He actually had a pretty good head on his shoulders. He had just invested entirely too much of his time into the wrong people, people who weren't doing anything good for themselves in their own lives.

We would ride around all day sometimes and get toasted off that good green. He'd sing to me, and even though he could not sing one tune, he made my day. It wasn't the fact that he was tone deaf that mattered; it was the fact that he was singing to me that made me feel special. And the way he called me his girl and bragged about me made me feel adored. Like he knew he had somebody who was worth it, and he wanted to make it clear that nobody else could have me. He was claiming me, and that was sexy as hell.

But, of course, the good times never lasted long. The other side of Corey would come out, and I hated him. This side was the "little boy" side of him, and this "little boy" had to give me fifty feet, for real. I could always tell when he was high on other shit, because he would wear the same clothes for days. He had no respect for me when he was lit up. His eyes would be bloodshot, and he couldn't hold on to his money for shit. The bad part of Corey came out more frequently than the good one. This demon stayed around a whole lot longer too.

The ugly truth about him was that he wasn't a real hustler. I mean, he hustled and had bread, but he would use that money to support his habit. He snorted powder, smoked wet, would lean off that snot, the whole damn nine. Mix all that shit together and what did you get? A true asshole by nature who didn't appreciate shit. When he was high, he didn't give a damn about anybody else but his no-good-ass friends. The saddest part of all, obviously, was that he didn't care two cents about his own self. I mean, how could he? All the drugs he was on, he was ruining himself. He might have looked good on the outside, but he was rotten on the inside.

He didn't blow all his money on his habit. That man stayed fresh to death from his head down to his toes. He'd walk in the club looking like he knew he was the finest thing in there. Most of the time he was. He would hustle to keep up with the Joneses. Always had to have the latest Jordans and gear to match.

Despite all that hatefulness he showed me, he gave me enough good for me to keep him around. The good was really what made me hang on to him. But I wanted only the good Corey, who treated me well, and not the bad one, who seemed like he hated me. We didn't always get what we wanted.

After the couple ahead of me gathered up their keys and coins, they headed toward the metal detector. I handed the heavyset guard my ID. I'd been there so many times, I already knew what to do.

"You're back again," she said to me as she wrote Corey's name down.

A lot of the guards who worked in the visitation area were beginning to recognize me, and some of them even greeted me by name. Now, if anybody else ever noticed that shit, they would think that it was a damn shame that these folks knew me on a first-name basis.

I smiled at the guard and finished signing in. She gave me the okay to walk through the metal detector. First, I placed the roll of quarters in my pocket and my truck keys on the tray, and then I strolled through the metal detector.

I caught a glimpse of myself as I headed past a mirror on my way to the seating area, which was nothing more than a dingy hallway with several plastic brown chairs lined up against both walls. I had curled my long hair, and soft curls now draped my smooth, paper sack–brown face. Some of the curls rested softly against my shoulders, and others flowed halfway down my back. I had on a pink-and-white sweater that clung tightly to my body.

I was wearing a pair of Mossimo jeans and had topped them off with brown riding boots that rested right above my knees. I gave myself a smile of approval. I knew my ass looked good.

I took a seat next to a Hispanic girl. We acknowledged each other with a nod of our heads and waited, along with several others, for someone to call out our loved one's name.

Some people wore their Sunday best. Others didn't care how they put themselves together, just as long as they abided by the Texas Department of Criminal Justice's dress code. A couple of people I recognized from previous Sunday or Saturday visits. The rest I hadn't seen before. As I sat in that dingy hallway, with nothing to occupy my mind, I played the guessing game again. Who were they coming to see?

Corey was currently serving a six-year sentence. He had already completed a year and a half. He had met with the parole board a couple of weeks ago, and we were waiting to see what the board had to say. Corey seemed to be doing extremely well in there. He had gotten his GED and was taking classes to get his carpentry certificate. He was also starting to realize what kind of "friends" he really had. None of his so-called friends had written him or come to see him once he left the county. His mom and his sister had been up there a couple of times. I guessed they were used to him being in and out of jail, and so they just visited whenever they felt like it.

I remembered the first time we met. He had just gotten out of jail when we crossed paths at the mall. That was when we locked eyes with each other. I guessed he liked what he saw as he watched me buy the latest pair of Jordan that had come out.

"Who you getting them Jordans for, little mama?" he asked as he walked up on me.

I was taken aback that he had approached me. I looked around and waved my hands in the air. "You don't see anybody around me, so obviously, they are for me."

"Oh, you feisty!"

"I'm not feisty. I just don't know any man wearing shoes this small," I said, defending myself.

I walked over to the counter to purchase my shoes, grabbing a bag of Nike socks in my size along the way. After paying for my shoes, I grabbed my bag, then turned around. He was still waiting on me. I smiled to myself. He was pretty cute. And that AKOO fit he was sporting was looking right on him. I tried to act like I didn't notice him when I walked by him.

"Can I get your name and number? I'd love to kick with you sometime, little mama. For real." He pulled his cell phone out and handed it over to me. I put in my number. The rest was history.

He hurried up and snatched me up that very same day. He took me off the market real quick. I soon found out how much different his world was from mine. He had no kids. He was an active member of One Tre Mafia, a Crips gang, and he banged often. He liked getting high, he liked fighting, and he loved that street life.

I, on the other hand, worked for one of the most renowned criminal defense attorneys in the city. Clip that. In all of West Texas. I was a secretary for Jerry Pine, attorney-at-law. He was the best defense attorney, and I personally wanted to be just as good as him one day.

When I saw that ad in the paper that he was looking for a secretary, I immediately jumped at the chance. He was looking for an experienced secretary, and I had to admit, I didn't have any experience. But I did have college credits and manager experience. And I was a people person. I won him over during my interview, and now I had been working for Jerry for almost two years.

I also had a son, Drake, who was now three. He was really my king, and he was my only child. A lot of people said he was spoiled, but I knew my son deserved the best, and he would get nothing less than that.

I leaned my head back and waited patiently for my turn. I caught a familiar face from the corner of my eye. I looked up to see a guy I'd known since middle school sweeping the floors. He was tall, dark, and handsome. Another African American guy was wiping the doors down. I noticed a guard was standing by the doors. He was supposed to oversee them, but he was busy joking around with one of the guards who worked in the check-in area. The guy I knew from way back when, the one who was sweeping the floor, noticed this too. He took that time to speak briefly with me.

"What's up, Doll?" He had a big grin plastered across his face.

"Hey. How are you?"

"Do you remember me? It's been a minute."

Of course I knew him. I smiled and nodded my head.

He started cheesing, focusing his attention back on the floor.

I looked at the guards who had struck up a conversation. They were still talking to one another. Neither one was paying attention to anything that was going on.

"What's up, Moses? What you doing in here?"

"That's a conversation to be saved for a time when I'm free."

"The families of Chase Lopez, Patrick Turner, Tommy Lozano, Frank Wright, and Corey Knight, come forward. They are waiting for you," I heard a female voice roar through the loudspeaker.

I couldn't help but smile as I stood up. I waved goodbye to Moses, then followed the crowd through the doors at the very end of the waiting area. We walked along another dingy-looking hallway, one in which lieutenants' pictures were on display. The TDCJ's dress code was also displayed on one wall, as were phone numbers to call if you suspected an inmate was suffering from abuse, neglect, and exploitation or if you weren't happy with the conditions of the prison and so on. That was bullshit to me. Why put up phone numbers in a damn hallway when visitors couldn't even bring a pen in to write them all down with? Common sense ought to tell them that!

I could see the double doors that loomed ahead in the dimly lit hallway. Bright lights shone from the two windows on the doors, and with each step I took, I could feel my face light up more with anticipation. I missed my nigga so much, and I could not wait to see him. It was obvious to me how close we were becoming. We were getting so emotionally connected, and I hoped that this didn't change when he touched down.

Once I walked past the double doors and entered the visiting area, I immediately noticed other inmates and their families. All the men were dressed in a white jumpsuit. Some had on black clog boots, and others had on blue strapped sandals. The only other differences were their skin colors and their tattoos. Some had tattoos on their face, neck, and arms, or even on all three. A lot of the inmates who were in the room today were white males. A couple of Mexicans were in there visiting, and there were four brothas.

A medium-sized square table separated the incarcerated men from their wives, parents, children, and friends. Only one hug and kiss before and after the visit was allowed, and you could hold hands. The incarcerated men couldn't get up to get their own snacks and drinks. You had to do that. They could excuse themselves to go to the restroom, but I figured nobody wanted to do that.

They wanted to savor every ounce of that two or four hours with family or friends they were getting that day, especially since they were surrounded by a bunch of men they didn't know or fuck with every single day. So fuck the bathroom. And I was sure they could hold it in too, if need be.

I scanned the room until my eyes finally met my boyfriend's. He had a table right smack in the middle of everybody, and I didn't give a damn. My heart fluttered and filled with excitement as I rushed over to him. With every step I took, his eyes smiled more, and finally, he rose eagerly from his seat. He wrapped his arms around me, pressed me tightly against him. Before I took a seat, I bought him a Lipton Iced Tea in a can and some Doritos. I got myself bottled water and some Rice Krispies Treats.

I placed everything down on the table. He grabbed my hands once I settled into my seat.

"What's up?" he asked me.

Corey was a mixed young man. He was black and white and had the prettiest brown eyes you'd ever seen. His smile was cunning, and he was taller than me.

I was five-three and had smooth brown skin, so I was the type of chick who complimented any man I was dating. I was very intelligent and well mannered. I was what you called a lady. For a young black woman, I was blessed with lengthy hair. I didn't have to wear a weave or tracks. In my town, where the haters lay, they liked to clown and say my hair was fusion weaved. I said, "Let them hoes think what they want," but they didn't hear me, though.

I had been a volleyball star back in my day and had done a lot of summer cross-country training to keep my wind up. Thanks to all that running, my thighs were thick as hell, as was that ass I sat on. Although I haven't touched a gym since before my son was born, my calves still served me well. Let's just say, I was right in all the places that mattered the most. I was petite, built just right, and had a very cute face. I wore a 32C cup size, but who wanted double Ds? Not me, so dismiss me with that one.

I smiled at my man. "Nothing much, love. Have you heard anything yet?"

He shook his head. "Any day now. I'm going crazy back there." He opened his bag of chips and ate one. His eyes never left mine. "I got it in the bag, though. The man that came and talked to me said he gonna recommend for me to come home."

"That's good," I said. I opened my water and took a sip.

"I ain't never had anybody who stayed around long enough like you have. You gonna be my wife, Dollie. For real." He smiled at me.

"Too bad I didn't sign that proxy. I could have been a Knight!" I joked with him. I laughed.

I remembered when he sent me that paper from the county. I'd been happy that day and the next. Then I'd got cold feet. Well, not really cold feet. My gut had told me not to do it, especially since he showed his ass our first six months together. I had got that shit bad, had wanted to ignore those feelings. Something had told me, though, *Do not pass go! Do not collect two hundred dollars.* Flashbacks of incidents that happened while he was using had kept flooding my mind. I'd decided he had to show me there was more to Corey than being a druggie and a drug dealer. So I hadn't done it.

Evidently, he thought that what I had said was funny, because he laughed right along with me. We continued our conversation, filling each other in on what had been going on in our lives. That was when I remembered my encounter with Moses up front.

"What happened to Moses? What's he doing in here?" I quizzed Corey.

"Ah, he got caught up in some bullshit. I can honestly say this time that it wasn't that nigga's fault why he locked up," Corey explained. "How you know he in here?"

"He was out there sweeping the floor," I said, taking a swig of my drink.

"Oh yeah. I forgot he switched jobs. He's in the same dorm as me. We always on the same team when we ball against them Dallas and Louisiana niggas."

Our two-hour visit flew by, and before I knew it, it was time to go. He stood up and pulled me close to him. He kissed me gently and played with my hair as we said our good-byes.

"I'll be home soon, Doll," he whispered in my ear. He kissed me one more time and then left to get his ID.

As I walked toward the double doors, we both turned around and waved to each other. Then he joined the line with the rest of the inmates who were headed back to their cells.

Chapter 2

Two weeks later . . .

"Jerry Pine, attorney-at-law," I said, greeting the caller on the other end of the line.

I was right in the middle of entering this week's payments from Jerry's clients into the computer. The one I was working on was seriously on the verge of being dropped as a client. He had made only one payment, and that was six months ago. But his mom had come in on Monday and had dropped off fifteen hundred dollars. All he owed now was about 750 dollars, which she had promised to pay by the end of next month.

Jerry was in the middle of three big trials. Two of them were murder cases, and the other one involved drug trafficking. He had been getting a lot of press from these cases and was working hard on them, on top of handling all the other cases, most of which were petty charges and weren't in the "limelight."

When he was busy like this, it was up to me to stay on top of things. He was a pricey attorney, and he had an eight-months rule. If clients hadn't been making steady payments within an eight- month period, he dropped them—with no refund. If they wanted to hire him back, they had to pay the remainder of what they owed up front. Depending on the case and the level of the offense, such as whether it was a first-degree felony and so on, that could easily range from twenty-five hundred to ten thousand dollars. As it turned out, a lot of people who had come in to pay this week were on the verge of being dropped.

A woman whose daughter was looking at thirty years for stabbing an abusive boyfriend to death had come in and paid four hundred dollars. It had been almost seven months since we'd seen her. She had already paid sixty-five hundred, and Jerry had taken the case for eight thousand. That was a lot of money to lose out on, and she was already so close to paying him off.

I wasn't a bill collector at all. It was Jerry's policy to send out two reminder notices. One at four months and one at six months. The final one advised the clients that they were about to be dropped. I went the extra mile and called them up and touched base with them as far as their payments went. My doing these reminder phone calls actually helped Jerry get his money.

Clients had to make sure their balance was paid in full before he would even represent them in court. If not, he'd push their court dates back to give them more time. But if he was not able to do that— or if he'd pushed the dates back too many times, to the point where he couldn't do it anymore—he'd drop them as clients. Jerry was very reasonable, and he was all about his money, but he loved proving his clients' innocence. Not to mention that this clean-cut blue-collar white man hated the DAs. Every single last one of them he could not stand, and that right there was the kind of lawyer you ought to be getting.

"What's up, big sis?" a cheerful voice answered back.

I immediately smiled at the phone and stopped typing. It was Corey's little sister, Naomi, calling me.

"It's about damn time!" I joked with her. "Have you heard from your brother?"

"Nah," she replied. "He ain't heard anything from the parole board yet?"

"Not as far as I know, he hasn't," I answered back.

We talked about it for a little while. I hadn't seen Corey in two weeks, and I was planning on going that weekend. I had been so caught up with helping Tammy, Jerry's paralegal, research some similar cases to help out with the major drug trafficking case that I had been too tired to make that drive. Not to mention, one of the weekends my son had been sick, so naturally, I had not dared leave my child. He came first. I knew that was something Corey would understand, because he had seen how I was about my son firsthand out here. He loved the way I treated my son and always complimented me for being such a good mom.

Naomi decided to meet me up at Formby. She had already made plans to go visit one of her aunts on their dad's side who resided in Lubbock, and so it made sense for her to go from there to the prison. I was excited because I knew Corey would love to see his sister. We both agreed to keep it a secret and just let him be surprised when he saw us all walk in. We talked a little while longer, and then I let her go.

It was almost three in the afternoon now, and I had to finish up posting these payments to everybody's accounts. Then I had to type up all the new case information for the two people Jerry had been speaking with over the past couple of months. They were still debating about who they wanted to represent them, and surprisingly, they had both come in and paid today. One had paid her first half up front, and the other girl had paid the initial six hundred dollars for him to get started researching the case.

I had just finished typing up the last person's information when Jerry and Tammy both walked in. Normally, Jerry went to court by himself, but with major cases, he liked for his paralegals to attend with him. He had once explained that he did this so that if his paralegals did pursue a career as a lawyer, they would know what to expect. With Jerry being in such high demand, some days I saw him, and other days I didn't. He worked on cases all over West Texas. Today, though, he had remained in Abilene all day, in court.

Tammy, his paralegal, had been with us for over a year. Whenever she didn't have to go to court with him, she did a lot of his interviewing for him. She went to the jails and prisons to talk to his clients, those who had either been court appointed to him or had been hired by loved ones.

He was a passionate attorney, and he treated everybody with the same amount of respect he showed someone who had never committed a crime. To him, you were innocent until proven guilty, and if he thought that you were guilty, he'd let you know up front, before you hired him. Even if he was court appointed, he'd tell you like it was.

Tammy wanted so much to be like him, so every time he had me schedule her for one of his court dates, she was super excited. She took his demeanor all in, because she wanted to represent her clients in that same respectful manner, but in her own style. She was currently going to Hardin Simmons and planned on attending graduate school in Houston the following school year or the year after that. Jerry had given her a good recommendation, as had a couple of other attorneys. Hell, one of the DAs had also given her a glowing recommendation letter, which she was ecstatic about. Jerry was proud about it too.

Tammy was a very fashionable white girl. She wore only name-brand clothes and often appeared snotty. But once you got the chance to know her, she was the most caring person you could ever come across. She was very tall and slim. Tammy had long, curly red hair. I knew a lot of redheads who hated their hair, but not this girl. She flaunted what she had and was proud of it.

It was almost time for me to close the office up to visitors, but Tammy had spared me this task. Upon entering, she had locked the office door behind her and had flipped the sign to CLOSED.

"How's it going?" she asked as she sat down. She turned on her computer so she could type up what had happened in court today from the notes she took.

"Nothing much." I gave her a recap of what had happened today, right down to Naomi's phone call.

"I'm glad you get along with your soon-to-be in-laws," she muttered. "If you didn't, that could end up being a nightmare in the long run."

I nodded my head in agreement. I offered my help to my coworker, but she declined. She was going to be there for another hour or so, and I probably would be a distraction to her.

I took the files for the new clients into Jerry's office and laid them on his desk. He was talking away on his phone, so I mouthed good-bye to him. He smiled at me and gave me two thumbs-up in the air. I smiled back as I exited his office, then got my things together.

Before I left, I said my farewells to Tammy. Outside, I hopped into my blue Toyota Tundra. Everybody said it was way too big for me. I didn't care. When I was in it, I felt like I was the biggest person, and I loved that I could drive that big ole truck with ease.

I headed down the street to the busy intersection. I was on my way to the north side to pick up my son from his day care. I loved the location where my son was at. The day care was in a little, secluded area and on its own block near downtown. Big trees hovered over the dark brown brick building, which took up half the block. The vans they transported kids in usually parked in front of the building. The rest of the block was the day-care's parking lot for the parents. The employees had reserved parking on both sides of the building. When you walked in, you could always count on the fresh smell of Pine Sol and a friendly face to greet you.

The day care was run by my aunt Audrina. She would have a fit if he attended any other facility but hers. Her day care held up to two hundred kids, who ranged in age from newborn to twelve years old. Each little classroom had a theme, and the one that my son was in was Noah's Ark. My aunt was big on education, nutrition, discipline, and manners. The parents loved my aunt because she had their kids saying, "No, ma'am" and "Yes, sir." They said grace before they ate, and they learned all kinds of songs. Starting with the age four groups, the providers were required to help the kids practice spelling their names and learn their colors, their ABCs, and their 123s. That was to assist especially the four-year-olds who had been unable to attend Early Head Start because their parents made too much.

She even had students from the three universities come in for a couple of hours in the afternoon to help the school-age kids out with their homework. She had a big outdoor playground that was gated, and those ten years old and up were taken on outings by their teachers, since their parents felt that they were too young to stay at home by themselves and too big to do a lot of the things the little kids did. She had her center on lock.

I picked up my son and shot over to my uncle's bakery on the way home. His bakery sat on the corner of one of the busiest streets in Abilene. He shared a facility with a grocery store, but the only way to enter was through the parking lot, not through the store. They had to close the original entrance off so they could extend the kitchen and the area they baked in. My uncle had had his shop for about ten years. His was a really good business, and he had got great ratings from the critics, the health department, and all three news stations.

I always stopped by my uncle's shop to get my son a big cookie. Drake enjoyed going there. Even though he always ended up with a big cookie, he liked to pretend he was having a hard time deciding what he wanted. Then my uncle would come through and say, "Drake! I got your cookie," causing my son to dissolve into a fit of chuckles. He liked to eat his treat with ice cream and got this delicacy almost every day.

My aunt Audrina and my uncle Justin were married. There were times when she would get off of work and would go and help him out. Sometimes, she would even stay and close down his store for him if he looked too tired.

Their youngest daughter, Victoria, also helped run the store. She was the closest to my age, but she was still older than me. My uncle Justin, of course, was black, and my aunt Audrina was a Mexican. Victoria was the youngest of six. She and her oldest sister, Cecily, had both taken more from the Mexican side. But the other four kids had taken more from the black side. Needless to say, all six of them could read, write, and speak fluent Spanish.

Victoria had always been their wild child and was quite spoiled. She didn't have a husband and wasn't blessed with any kids. She had once been heavily dependent on cocaine. Sometimes, she had done well when she was using; other times, she hadn't. For a long time, nobody had known that she was even on that shit. There had been times when we would see Victoria on a regular basis, and there had been times that we wouldn't see her or hear from her in days. My aunt and uncle were used to it. When she would finally come around, she would look so sickly thin.

She would come up with the excuse that she had been sick and just hadn't felt like bothering anybody. That was an easy story to believe since Victoria had frequented the doctor's office ever since she was young. She was the child who had ended up sick with any and everything. They naturally believed she really had been ill and would scold her for not calling.

I was the first one to find out that Victoria was a smoker. I found this out before Corey went to jail. Corey and I had been lounging around the house we shared at the time. One of his homeboys had come over, and they'd gone into the bathroom. Whenever they did that, I knew that my sweet boyfriend was leaving the house and a prick was going to emerge from that bathroom. That left a bitter taste in my mouth. Sure enough, that day the Devil came out of the bathroom, with bloodshot eyes and a runny nose.

Whatever he'd snorted must have been some pretty strong shit. Both boys came out walking into each other. They were running into the walls and shit. Had goofy looks plastered on their faces. Corey demanded that I dropped them off in the hood. I did not hesitate to grab my keys and take them. The sooner Corey got away from me, the better I'd be.

On the way to their neighborhood, Corey received a phone call on his cell. He had me take him to hit a lick. I didn't think twice about it. I did it to avoid an argument. If I had told him no, then things wouldn't have ended well. Not long after I pulled up to a well-known, run-down, shabby-looking crack house, I saw my cousin stumble out of the house to meet him. If she saw my truck, she didn't give a damn. She just wanted to hit that shit my awful boyfriend had.

Victoria looked distraught. Her normally well-kept curly hair was matted to her face and neck. Although they were over six feet away, a horrible stench insulted my nose. I couldn't tell if it was body odor, rotten eggs, or something like a dead body but not quite. My cousin looked dirty and wore a blue polo dress and some flip-flops. This nigga Corey knew she was my family, and he was sellin' to her, anyway. I should have left his ass right fuckin' then, but I didn't. I should have told my aunt and uncle she was getting fucked up off that shit then, but I didn't. I should have intervened in the whole thing, but I just didn't.

The memories of seeing her show up at her parents' house after no one had seen her for three weeks came rushing back to me. That was because right then and there, I realized she was on a rock star binge. She was so bad that she used to rent out her Excursion, which my uncle had gotten her, for days at a time in exchange for crack. My aunt and uncle paid her rent and bills faithfully, not realizing that their child was on something.

One Sunday when she showed up from one of her disappearing acts, which were starting to become quite frequent, a sheriff knocked on their door. They arrested my cousin for shoplifting at several different stores around town. My aunt tried hard to defend her. They had her on tape stealing with another girl. The other girl got caught in Dillard's, and when she was apprehended, she gave up Vic.

It was within several weeks of her arrest that the truth about my cousin hit my aunt and uncle. They went to her apartment to clean it out and move everything into storage. They found empty mechanical pencils and foil in the inside of her car. Inside her apartment, they found several things that they suspected she had cooked the coke up with. Her apartment reeked. I recognized that smell since I had experienced it the day I saw her at that crack house. She had no clean clothes or food.

My aunt broke down and cried when she found used condoms and condom wrappers all over her bedroom and living-room floors.

On top of that, Victoria had confessed to them that when she hit up the stores, she was heavily under the influence. She was trading sex for a hit. She was letting anybody use her SUV for an eight ball right down to crumbs, and she was constantly boosting and selling to continue to support her habit.

The confession hurt her parents terribly. My wonderful boss was able to get her three years deferred adjudication probation. But under the watchful eye of my uncle, she had to complete rehab. First, she had to agree to go to, and then she had to complete it successfully in order for her probation to begin. She agreed, and the judge approved her sentence.

She went to St. Judes Recovery for Women, a private center, and she completed her twelve-step program in nine months. When she finished the program, she looked heavier, healthier, and astonishingly beautiful. She knew with help, she would be fine. She found a sponsor who wasn't too far from Abilene. The couple who sponsored her actually lived in Clyde. Both were recovering drug addicts and had been clean for eleven years. They kept up with her and her meetings on a regular basis.

Her probation officer checked on her and even gave my cousin her cell phone number, just in case Vic ever found herself in a bind or on the verge of a relapse. She was blessed to have an adult probation officer who really cared. She understood what Vic was going through due to losing her own brother to drugs.

So, here my crazy cousin was, helping my uncle run his bakery, looking livelier than ever. She normally was the one who did the baking if my uncle had his hands full.

She also trained the employees to bake. She was adorable but feisty as hell. One thing that had never changed about her was that she was always in somebody's business . . . especially mine.

Chapter 3

Drake and I walked into the bakery. There weren't too many people in the shop. The people who had already been helped were just waiting to be checked out. My uncle Justin was assisting the customers, and one of his employees was ringing them up. Another employee was the runner. He helped make sure that the store looked clean and the displays were full. I could see Victoria and another baker through the window of the door to the kitchen. Victoria was busy rolling out dough, and the other baker was applying chocolate frosting to a chocolate cake.

Drake made a beeline toward the cookies, and on cue, my uncle Justin was there, giving him a hard time.

"Young man, I can't give you a chocolate chip cookie. But we got some dough in the back. You can make your own," he offered jokingly to his great nephew.

"Nope!" A bullheaded Drake shook his head and stood firm. "I want my cookie now, Unna Jushi!"

My uncle teased him for a little longer and then gave him his cookie with ice cream. We said our good-byes and climbed into my truck.

Once we arrived at my aunt and uncle's house, where Drake and I lived, I unlocked the door. The neighborhood they resided in was very busy. Everybody looked after one another. Tons of kids rode their bikes up and down the streets. Somebody was always barbecuing or having people over. Older adults sat outside and gossiped. Some people simply watched the neighborhood from their lawn chairs.

The place I called *home* was the nicest residence on the block. It was a four-bedroom home and had a huge kitchen. My aunt's entire house was decorated in an Italian theme. Even the outside of her place reminded you of a diminutive Italy house, with its elevated arches and its numerous slender windows.

My aunt had chosen a very tan color for the exterior, with a heavy brown as the accent color, when it came time to paint the house. Exotic flowers embellished the front of the house. They were gorgeous, but they had thorns all over them, so you couldn't pick them. With their deep reds and dark blues, they looked great against the house.

My uncle was my mom's oldest brother, and when she was killed when I was a child, he helped my dad's mom look after me. All my aunts and uncles turned flaky toward me when my mom was murdered in a robbery. When I say flaky, I mean they would say they were going to help out but then would never come through. You know, empty promises a deadbeat dad or mom would say to children. Except the difference was I wasn't their child. They clearly didn't want to be bothered with me, either. My dad had been incarcerated pretty much all my life. His mom stepped up to the plate and took me in. She took care of me with Uncle Justin's and Aunt Audrina's help, even though they had their own kids to tend to. They came to my volleyball games and invited me and my grandma to their house for holidays. She invited them for Easter and the Fourth of July.

My grandma died of a massive heart attack a couple of years before I had my son. And naturally, my aunt and uncle stepped in to help, just as they had when I was a child. Before long they invited me to move in with them.

I unlocked the front door and settled my son at the kitchen table so he could eat his cookie and ice cream. He had already had spaghetti at the day care, which my aunt had fixed for him. I quickly ran outside to check the mail.

There were bills for my aunt and uncle and a letter from Corey to me. I sat outside as I opened it, positioning myself so I could see Drake through the windstorm screen door. I stared at Corey's nice handwriting on the envelope before I opened the letter.

Once I had ripped the letter open, I noted that he was still whining about the visits he hadn't received the past couple of weekends. He also let me know he had made parole and was probably going to leave that unit soon. He had a sixty-day setback, which meant he'd be a free man in two months.

I immediately ran inside and dialed Brenda's number. She was Corey's mom. Although we had never met, she already seemed to approve of me. She liked that I worked, and she liked that I had goals. I wasn't into partying and going clubbing on a regular basis. But, of course, there were times when I would step out. Whenever Corey would start acting out and trippin' while he was on his drugs, and whenever we had a bad argument, I'd call her.

For the life of me, I could never understand why he was the way he was. I wasn't dumb. I knew that people who did drugs were dependent on them for a reason. But what was his excuse? I needed Brenda to be aware of how screwed up he was acting. We all knew what direction he was headed in. He knew it as well, but I figured he didn't care or he was wildin' out just because. One minute he wanted to be a man, and the next he acted like a child who could not be disciplined.

I had never even seen a picture of his mom, but I knew she was white. I also knew that she had to be a strong and beautiful woman. Naturally, she cared about her son, but what could you do when he wouldn't listen to you? I didn't think he understood how much he had hurt her. When he got locked up, it affected a lot of people, and while listening to some of his childhood stories from her mouth, I could hear the pain in her voice.

When I got her voice mail after my third attempt at calling, I left her a message. Then I debated whether or not to call Naomi. She truly loved her big brother, and that was evident.

Naomi was a little off, and although she meant well, she had way too much drama going on in her own life. In the pictures I had seen of her, she looked like her brother, but she had long, curly hair. She was described to me as a manipulator. I just saw her as a young girl who needed to make mistakes to learn her way. Find her position in life. I was not sure if all the mistakes she was making were necessary, but who was I to judge?

I decided not to call Naomi, but I did called Corey's brother, Tiger. Either way, I knew one of them would call her and fill her in. I just didn't want her to make a big deal and blow everything out of proportion. It was best to let the brothers control all of that.

Tiger's wife picked up the phone, and after I let her know who I was, I explained to her what was going on. She let me know that she would tell Tiger as soon as he arrived back from his Little League baseball practice. We spoke for a little while longer; then we disconnected with each other.

Now, his brother was more my variety of people. He was totally different than his younger siblings. He was working on his master's in psychology and was very family oriented. He was built more like their dad. He actually resembled his dad more. Corey often described him as a square, but I didn't see anything squarish about a man trying to provide a brighter future for his family. If anything, Corey should look up to him and follow in his footsteps. But it was what it was.

A few minutes later Corey's mom called me back. I ran through the whole spiel with her as well. She was so happy, she was crying. Then it turned real serious.

"Doll, I really hope that you guys consider moving down this way," she said, with a hint of hope in her voice.

"Yes. Naomi actually discussed all that with me. We are going to bring up that idea to him here pretty soon, when we meet up at Formby."

"Yeah, she told me about it. I want to believe this time he will come." Sadness was pouring out through the phone. I couldn't help but feel for the poor woman. "All I want is for my son to be able to have a good life with the people who care about him. The streets don't love nobody."

I couldn't agree with her more.

We chatted for a little while longer. Really, I listened more than talked. Once she was done venting, we hung up. Despite how his mom was feeling, I was thrilled. The wait was nearly over. My baby would soon get out, and we could finally be together again.

Chapter 4

That Saturday, I met Naomi at the prison. We both were going to see Corey together. Naomi and I had become acquainted before Corey got locked up. This whole year and a half had brought me closer to his family. His parents were divorced. His dad lived here with his grandma, whom I had also grown close to. His mom, his sister, and his brother all resided in Bedford, a suburb of Fort Worth.

My opinion of her went like this: she was the annoying little sister. She was slightly taller than me and had a light complexion. Her hair was dark brown, naturally curly, and rested on her shoulders. She was slightly thicker than me. Unlike her brother, who had a thug-like swag, Naomi talked like she was a Valley girl. She carried herself like a rich white girl and dressed in all the latest fashions. She never wore the same thing twice. But when this girl got rowdy, the nigga inside her emerged.

She had a precious little girl named Nestle. Nestle looked just like Corey to me. Her smile was wickedly beautiful, and that part of her came from her uncle Corey. She had dark red hair with a hint of blond. Her thick, curly hair flowed down her back and complemented her complexion, which was slightly darker than her mom's. Although Naomi was fond of her daughter, her mind frame was still stuck in her childhood. She often left Nestle for days at a time with her mom or Tiger. But she always came back, so I guessed that was good.

Naomi was already there waiting on me when I pulled my truck into the visitors section. I had brought my son, Drake, with me. Drake had grown pretty fond of Corey. We both wanted their relationship to continue to grow.

"Hey, Dollie! Hi, Drake!" Naomi greeted us.

Nestle had not quite woken up from her nap, and Naomi was carrying her. Drake smiled up at Naomi as we walked into the building and got in line so we could sign in to see Corey.

"Mom and I were talking," Naomi was saying. "We both really want Corey to come to Bedford."

"I think he should go too, but I know he won't go without us," I said to her.

Naomi turned toward me, shifting her child's head from her left to the right shoulder. "We want you and Drake to come. We just feel like he would do better in Bedford rather than in Abilene."

I had to agree with her on that. Corey and I had often talked about what could happen when he got out. Sometimes, I even got a bad feeling about what would happen when he got out, but I didn't know why I had this bad feeling, and I would just push it to the back of my mind. I ignored this feeling because Corey seemed so sincere. I also trusted him.

We chatted about the move until it was time for us to sign in. When we were finished, we walked through the metal detector and waited for them to call Corey's name.

Once again, Moses was out sweeping the floor. Instead of the African American, a short Mexican man was wiping the floor and the windows down. A black lady correctional officer was supervising them. Her eyes were glued to both of them. Moses didn't dare look up or speak. I wasn't upset by it.

We waited patiently for almost thirty minutes. They called Corey's name, and we followed the crowd into the visiting room. My boyfriend had gotten us a table at the back of the room. Once he saw all of us, his eyes lit up. I knew he was happy to see us, especially Naomi and his niece, who hardly ever came to see him.

As everybody took their seats, I went to the snack machines and got our food. I also got our drinks as well. I took my seat and began passing out the drinks. I noticed that Drake had taken a seat on Corey's lap. I also noticed that Nestle had woken up. Corey's sister was pitching her idea to him, and Corey seemed to be listening very closely to her. I gave my drink and chips to Nestle and went to get myself some more. When I came back, I took a seat and Corey grabbed my hands.

"You know I made parole, right?" he asked me. "You got my letter?"

I nodded at him. I opened my water bottle and took a sip. "Where did you parole to?"

"I think my granny's address. But, say, we gonna move to Bedford. I'd do better down there than in Abilene." He took a sip of his soda. He rubbed my hand with his free hand.

Naomi grabbed my hand, squealing like a pig. I traded smiles with her crazy ass. She squeezed my hand as she grinned real big at her older brother.

"What about your friends, though? Did your homies in the hood not keep money on your books or something?" she teased sarcastically.

"Fuck them niggas. They ain't wrote me or nothin' since I got here. I made it this far without them, so I can keep going."

Naomi and I traded smiles with each other again. The rest of the visit flew by, as usual, and we all said our tearful good-byes before our departure. Afterward, Naomi and I stood in the parking lot and talked for a few minutes before we left the premises.

"My brother really loves you," Naomi said.

I looked at her.

"I hope you guys move down there. Corey always says he's gonna do right. He always gets out, fucks up, and goes right back in."

I knew she saw the stunned expression on my face, because she laughed it off.

"Maybe he will do right by you," she added, then walked in the direction of her car, Nestle in tow.

"He better," I thought aloud as Drake and I returned to the truck.

The ride back home never took as long as the drive up there. We were back in Abilene within a couple of hours. I decided to swing through Corey's old neighborhood to talk to his dad and his grandma. I hadn't gotten a chance to let them know he was on his way home.

When I pulled into their driveway, both Granny Gina and his dad, Michael, were already outside. Granny Gina's face lit up when my truck pulled in. I hopped out and went to let my son out. When I released him, he ran toward her and gave her legs a big hug.

"Got any news for me?" Michael was sitting on the bench outside Granny Gina's brick house. He was smoking a cigar and had a forty in his hand.

Michael was a tall, dark-skinned black man who towered over you when he stood. I had never thought to ask him, but I knew he was well over six feet. He had an athletic build, and despite the beer belly he was growing, you can tell he was into sports.

Michael had been a basketball and track star back in his day. He'd pursued a college education on a basketball scholarship. That was when he had met Corey's mom, down in El Paso. At the time, Brenda had been working as a librarian part-time and had been going to school to try to become a teacher. However, after they got together, she soon got pregnant with Tiger and dropped out. Michael continued his education and went on to become a basketball coach.

According to Corey, they had lived all over Texas and hadn't really wanted for anything. But, for some reason, his parents had split up. Michael had moved in with his mom, and Brenda had moved to Fort Worth. Since then it had been a battle between the two. For a long time, Corey had been concerned because his mom wanted him there with her. But Corey had always wanted to be with his dad and Grandma Gina.

"Corey made parole," I let them both know. I took a seat next to Corey's dad.

"Where he parole to?" his grandma asked. She held Drake's hands, and he swung them back and forth.

Grandma Gina was a short, chunky, light-skinned elderly woman. She moved with swiftness and talked with a thick Jamaican accent. Grandma Gina wasn't Jamaican, but her deceased husband had grown up in Jamaica. Throughout her life being married to Mr. Knight, she had spent plenty of time on the island. Even after his passing, she would often take trips down there. I guessed once the accent grew on her, it just never left her.

I shrugged my shoulders. "All I know is he's coming here, but he wants to move to Bedford," I said to them.

They both started laughing.

"That nigga there got some decisions to make when he gets out," Michael said. "If he doesn't straighten his ass out, he's going back."

"Don't you get a place with him until he gets a job," Granny Gina told me. "If things are going to work, he has to show you he can be a man, honey."

She was right about that.

Michael leaned over and stretched his long legs out. He took a big sip from his forty. "I know one thing is for sure. You are too damn good for him, Dollie. Don't put up with his shit, either. You watch and see. His ass gonna fuck up and go right back if his ass don't get some damn act right."

Chapter 5

I was able to see Corey two more times before they put him on the transfers. He was sent to Middleton. From there, he went to Mineral Wells, and then he finally ended up at this trustee camp outside of San Antonio. I had been calling the parole office every week. I finally learned he was getting out on August 18. That was less than a week away.

I felt restless as I waited for the eighteenth to roll around. I wanted Corey to have some new clothes, so I got him two pairs of Jordans, plenty of outfits to match, and a couple of hats. I also got him a toothbrush, boxers, deodorant, and plenty of things like that. I could not wait for him to come home.

When his release date finally arrived, I was all over the place. I had to keep myself preoccupied at work. His mom was calling me all the time. His sister and his brother were too. His friend Drew also came by my job twice to see if Corey had hit me up.

Drew happened to be one of the only friends that Corey had that I approved of. He was polite and nice. He banged too, but he normally kept to himself. Drew was also one of the sexiest guys I'd ever laid eyes on. He was Dominican and black. He had the creamiest tan skin, and it made you want to reach out and lick all over it. He dated a girl named Koa Grace. I disliked the girl, but Drew was cut for her, and out of respect for him, I never dissed her to his face. But I did advise him to seek better females.

When Drew stopped by the second time, he had on a black shirt with Tupac on it, a pair of nicely creased and heavily starched jeans, and a pair of black Nike Air Maxs. He looked rather nice to me. Nobody was in the office but me that day. Around two o'clock, Tammy had left for the day, and Jerry had court dates in San Angelo and Comanche. I was pretty sure I wasn't going to hear from him, let alone see him at all that day. When Drew came in, I was busy typing up Jerry's case summaries and his opening acts for three of his court appearances tomorrow.

"Hey, Dollie." Drew smiled at me.

He made my heart melt a little. I had to remind myself that Drew was Corey's friend.

"What's up, Drew!" I greeted cheerfully.

He took a minute to check me out. I was sure of that. I had my hair pulled back into a ponytail, showing off the length of it. I had chose to wear a pin-striped dress suit with a black vest today. I had my black doll heels on. I knew I looked fine that day. To my satisfaction, Drew thought so too. When he noticed I was watching him check me out, he smiled at me, embarrassed. I laughed at him.

"It's all good, Drew. You ready for Corey to get out?" I said.

"You still haven't heard from him?" he asked, leaning against my desk.

I shook my head no.

"You guys will stop by my house, right?"

I nodded my head yes. I flashed him a smile.

He said his good-byes, and I smiled back before he left.

As I had predicted, Jerry called to let me know he wouldn't be back in the office today. I got the materials he needed for his court date in Brownwood together so I could leave them in the mailbox at his house. I locked up the office and left to pick up my son.

After I picked him up, I dropped off Jerry's papers at his house. Then I took Drake to get a Coke float from an ice cream parlor around the corner from my boss's house. I let him drink his float there, and then we headed home.

When I pulled into the driveway, I noticed that both my aunt's and uncle's cars were there. Right when I walked in the door, I heard my aunt talking on the phone.

"So, when did you get out?" I heard her say.

I knew it was Corey. I hurried and snatched the phone from her. "Bye, Corey!" she shouted.

I headed down the hall, toward my bedroom. I heard Drake chatting my aunt's head off, so I knew he was all right.

"Where are you?" I demanded as I closed my bedroom door.

I heard him laugh. "Two and a half hours away. We've been stuck in Fredericksburg on a furlough for almost four hours now." He paused. "I can't wait to be with my wife," he added softly.

His voice brought comfort to my heart. I was head over heels in love with Corey, and he knew it.

"Can't wait, either, babe," I whispered to him.

He told me to be at the bus stop at 9:45 p.m. I assured him I'd be there.

"Wear something sexy," he said.

He knew I would too.

Chapter 6

Tenosha

"Ten, I'm back!" Bobbie called out.

I heard the kids running through the hall to greet him. I barely lifted my head up. I was right in the middle of my nap, and this damn fool was calling out for me. I heard Hanson and Marie mumbling something. I figured they were telling him about their day at school, like they did every single day, after he got off of work. I was dead tired and wanted more than anything to fall back asleep. No matter how hard I tried to block their tiny voices out, though, I just couldn't.

I slowly rose from the bed. I decided that I might as well cook before Bobbie started his bitchin'. He always complained if his dinner wasn't ready by a certain time. I didn't know what the fuck his ass thought this was, but this wasn't the fuckin' fifties. I damn sure wasn't his mama, either. I had given him four children, and I still didn't have a ring. So housewife duties, a homemade lunch to take to work, dinner on the table, hot bathwater run for him, or whatever bullshit he was expecting, he was not about to get from me. If he was looking for a woman to be a slave, like his mama was to his daddy, he had better not look to me. Ain't no slave over here.

Shit pissed me off just thinking about it. Bobbie and I had been together for years. The beautifully mixed children we had made together were perfect to us. I had to admit, the first three kids had come during our high school years. The last one had arrived six days after graduation.

I actually had it made. I didn't have to go punch a clock at somebody's business at all. He did that, and he took care of everything else too. Once it came to us, though, there was nothing. There was no passionate kissing, no "Baby, this" or "Baby that," no excitement to see one another. It was like the butterflies were nonexistent. I guess the best way to put it was that the attraction wasn't there anymore. We never did anything together, hardly talked, and I guessed we just stuck it out for the kids' sake.

I slid my bright yellow pedicured toes into my black house shoes. I got up and made the bed. I quickly combed my curly hair and arranged it in a bun, wrapping it tightly with a blue bandanna. I walked out of the bedroom and then stood in the hallway for a minute. I inhaled deeply, preparing myself for a verbal battle, before I started to stroll down the hall to the kitchen.

Bobbie was lounging in the recliner in the living room with our three-year-old son, Tyrese, on his lap. Our son was preoccupied with playing a game on his father's tablet. My one-year-old, Karen, was holding on to Bobbie's leg and singing the words "ole McDonald" over and over again. Hanson, my oldest son, was showing Bobbie his schoolwork. Marie, my second oldest, was sprawled on the arm of his chair. They all seemed content but crowded. I was relieved. He could deal with their bad asses. While Bobbie treated me far from good, he was an excellent father and was loving when it came to our kids

Bobbie was white but had naturally tanned skin, and his eyes were brown. He could easily pass for a light-skinned Mexican with the way he kept his hair shaved.

Not skinhead shaved, but lower, like that of a cholo. He had grown up in a black neighborhood, around nothing but niggas. He might look like a white boy, but his swag and the way he talked were anything but that.

Bobbie's parents weren't too fond of me. They had always said I tried to trap his ass. His mom couldn't stand me. She used to say some rude, disrespectful shit, like he could do better than me. That if he was going to date outside his race, he should date a full black girl with good home training. That shit insulted the hell out of me too. I despised that ho with a passion, just like she couldn't stand a glimpse of me.

His father had warmed up to me over the years. He had actually taken the time to get to know me as a person. He knew more about my family and our background than Bobbie's mom did. I used to wonder how a nice man like him would link up with a bigoted prude like her ass. If anybody was too good for anybody, it was him being too good for her. She was able to keep him only because she was OCD and kept their house spick and span. She stayed in the kitchen, baking and cooking, trying to feed everybody's love. Fuck that. That shit wasn't me.

Both of his parents were hardworking people. They had just known that Bobbie was going to go to college on a baseball scholarship. When Bobbie and I first met, they said I was ruining his life. Little did they realize that even though he'd got the scholarship, he didn't have the grades. And if they did know his grades sucked, they didn't dare mention anything about it. Especially his mom. She wouldn't dare get caught looking like a fool, since her Bobbie was a baseball star.

I remembered when she found out what he was really doing at school. See, Bobbie would go to first period for five minutes, and then he would ditch the rest of the day to hit the block. His head got real fucking big once he stacked his first ten Gs. That was what first attracted me to him. He was a go-getter, a hustler. He spent all his money on me, constantly showering me with gifts. I really loved him with my all.

He never wanted me to be with him when he hustled. Although his parents were batting against us, back in those days, we were inseparable, until he went to make his money. By the time I was carrying our third child, he had given the game up and had traded that lifestyle in for a work suit.

He had claimed he didn't want his kids to grow up having to visit their pops in a prison somewhere. Or even having to go visit his grave site. That was around the time one of his closest friends was carjacked, robbed, and found dead in Dallas. All this guy was supposed to do was meet their connect, but he got set up instead. Crazy part about that situation, Bobbie was supposed to meet with the connect at the same time. He ended up having to stay behind with me due to Hanson cutting his thumb while playing outside at a neighbor's house. Our son came running full speed toward his daddy, screaming and crying as blood leaked from his hand.

It was so bad, we couldn't tell which finger it was. The ambulance was called. Right then Bobbie made that decision to ride with his son, and so his homeboy left alone for Dallas. Don't get me wrong. Even though Bobby didn't hustle anymore, he still banged hard with One Tre. He just left the dope game completely alone after the loss of his friend.

Bobbie and I had been together for eight years. He was twenty-one and had an all right job working for Pepsi. It was all right because I didn't have to work. I was nineteen years old, with four kids, and I had my own house. I was a mixed bitch. I was half black and Dominican. So Bobbie's skin tone mixed well with mine, and our kids were a beautiful mix, with a variety of light-skinned complexions. The girls looked like they could pass for white youngsters, but the firm ringlets that covered their tiny heads gave away the fact that they had niggas in their bloodline.

Hanson looked more Mexican than anything. If anything, that little nigga right there favored my younger brother, Drew, who kept his own hair faded, but when it grew out, his natural curls made him look even more like a Mexican. Hanson was the darkest one out of the four kids.

My youngest son's complexion was closer to mine, but like his older brother, he looked like a Mexican. My mom and them would get pissed if you referred to the boys as Mexicans, since their nationality was Dominican. We weren't Mexicans at all, but even I could see where people were coming from with that.

Of all the children, my youngest son, Tyrese, was the one that you could tell just by looking at him that his ass had to be mixed with black. His hair was more on the kinky side. His face resembled those on my dad's side. He shared the big nose, the big lips, and the big head. He was the odd child, but when all of them were together, you could tell they were mine and Bobbie's.

My kids were also bilingual and knew Spanish, thanks to my mom and grandma. They shocked the whole neighborhood when they started speaking that Spanish. They were smart too and could tell if you knew what they were saying. Just like the Chinese women at the nail shop who talked shit about your toes, they were quick to talk that shit in Spanish. People would laugh, not realizing they were making fun of them.

After seeing that the kids were occupied with their father, I hurried into the kitchen and cleaned up. I washed the dishes and wiped the counters off. By the time I got ready to put my meat loaf together, my daughter Marie came in to help.

"Your mom didn't comb your hair today," I heard Bobbie say to Karen.

I rolled my eyes. He had better not start that bullshit today, 'cause I'd make his white ass cry like the bitch who pushed his ass out of her at birth. Bobbie wanted beef, and I was going to deliver him the whole cow if he started tryin' to fuck with me.

"Your ass won't work, so the least you can do is make my kids look presentable," I heard him yell out.

"Shut the fuck up!" I yelled back.

"For real, though, Ten. The fuck you do all damn day?"

"Maintained this house and watched your fuckin' kids. The fuck you think I did?"

I could feel my body start to shake with anger. I stood holding on to the sink, waiting for him to say something else smart. I was ready to go upside his head again. The most he had ever done to me in retaliation was pin me down to the floor until I calmed down. Normally, by the time he got me on the floor, I'd given him two or three knots across his fuckin' forehead. I was ready to bust his nose today, though.

When I realized he was not going to have shit else to say, I decided to get back to cooking. I swore before God that if I didn't have these children, I wouldn't be in this kitchen, trying to cook up some shit.

Marie and I finished preparing the sides. I went to sit at the kitchen table while the meat loaf cooked. I had Marie go get my cell phone off the charger. I watched from the corner of my eye as Bobbie complained out loud about the way the living room looked. Karen and Tyrese had brought out every toy they could find and had them scattered all over the living-room floor. I didn't care. He just better be glad he was getting dinner. He was off work now, so he could pick that shit up his damn self. I knew he was trying to bait me into another conversation, but fuck that dude. I just ignored his offenses.

Marie ran back with my cell phone. I gave her a kiss, followed by a monster-sized hug. She dissolved into a fit of giggles. I patted her on the butt and instructed her to go play while dinner was cooking. She obliged.

I called my grandma's house. I wanted to know if a letter had come from a friend of mine. My homeboy Corey was locked up and had been writing me for the past six months. I'd always been attracted to Corey but had never got at him. I had always had my man, and he continuously kept a different girl or two.

He wrote me from time to time, and I always sent a letter back. I hadn't gotten mail from him in a couple of weeks, but that was customary. Corey went with this stuck-up bitch named Dollie Benson. It was all good, though. He had a girl, and I had a man, even though I didn't give a fuck about mine at that moment. I feel like if an opportunity with Corey ever developed again, I would jump on it. Regardless of who got mad or offended.

"Grandma?" I asked when she finally answered.

"Yes, mija?" she replied.

"Did I get any mail?"

She told me no. I conversed with her for a good fifteen minutes, then hung up the phone.

Right then, my sister, Justine, accompanied by her husband, Bruce, waltzed into the house. Instantaneously, Bobbie's tone of voice changed, and he challenged Bruce to a game on the Xbox. I rolled my eyes again. It irritated me how quickly he turned fake in front of company.

"What's up, Ten?" Justine asked, taking a seat at the kitchen table.

I shrugged my shoulders. I was a little bummed that Corey hadn't written. I just wanted to stew in my mood until it was time to take the meat loaf out and make the kids' plates.

Justine was my younger sister. She was a bit darker than me, but we both stood at about the same height. I was larger than Justine, due to my babies and all that drink I would sip on. She had a smaller frame. Yeah, I was a big girl compared to her, but don't let the heaviness fool ya. I had a pretty face, and I knew I was still fine, big or not.

Justine and my brother Drew favored each other more. They both took after the black side, whereas I took after the Dominican side. They both shared the same skin. Justine had thick, wavy hair, which she kept pulled back in a ponytail. She had a heavier Spanish accent than me, and when my sister got mad, she was livid. She wasn't scared of anybody, but she avoided drama as much as she could. Once you pushed her buttons, however, she went senseless.

Drew was the same exact way. He was more on the quiet side and didn't really associate with too many individuals outside One Tre Mafia. He was tall and kept his head faded. Sometimes, he would let his hair grow out. His curls were too thick and uncontrollable, so he rarely would do that. My brother stayed clean cut and always rocked the latest Air Force 1s and Jordans. He was always on the block, hustling.

He had a girlfriend named Koa, and I couldn't stand her ho ass. This woman was a thin, pretty, dark-skinned chick who was always put together. She always rocked the latest Coach bags, designer clothes, and heels. You never caught her without heels on, ever. She was always finding boots and sneakers that had heels. She displayed the latest hairdos. Koa always kept her toes and finger-nails done as well.

Truth be told, though, that bitch was very dramatic—insane, really. She was branded for acting like a clown with whatever nigga she dated. She had done off-the-wall shit, stunts like trying to run her boyfriends' asses over, stabbing them with knives, and other stupid, childish shit like that. I heard she was bipolar and was supposed to be taking medication for it. But, no matter what, my brother loved that senseless female, so I stomached her. If he liked it, I loved it.

The best thang about my little brother was that he always had money. If I needed it, my brother had it. Even when I didn't think he had it, he always did. That was my one and only baby bro, and I loved him terribly.

Justine lowered her voice a little. "Did you hear about Corey?" She knew I was writing him, using Grandma's address.

I shook my head no.

"Corey's getting out today."

Chapter 7

It had been two weeks since Corey's release, and I hadn't seen or heard from his ass. I wasn't disappointed, but the least the nigga could have done was holla at me.

I had just taken the kids over to Bobbie's parents' house. They wanted to take the kids for the weekend, and I was happy. Majesta, Justine, Bruce, Bobbie, and I were going to go out that night.

Majesta was my best friend. She was younger than me, but she was still my girl. She always had my back. My bestie was a banana-colored black girl. She could be a supermodel due to her tall, slender shape. She had a pretty smile and always wore tracks in her hair. Majesta was young and always dated whatever nigga was on at the moment. However, at that moment, my girl was single, and she was ready to bag the next dope boy making bread. A lot of people hated on her and said she was the neighborhood ho. To me, though, she was a kindhearted person and rode hard for her friends and family. She was always fighting, and she was always high off of something, mainly weed or pills. But she was my bitch.

My brother Drew called to see if we were going out. He was planning on meeting us there. I told him where we were going. I gave Bobbie the phone so he could talk to him.

Majesta and Justine were in the bathroom, putting on their makeup. I joined them in front of my long mirror, which covered almost half of the bathroom wall. I squeezed in between the two of them so I could run some mousse through my curls.

"Bobbie's coming with us, and I just got done telling Majesta that Corey and Dollie are supposed to be there," my sister told me.

"He's going with that bitch?" I made a face while I put the mousse evenly through my curls.

"He's just using her. Watch, he gonna fuck her over and fuck with you. I know my big bro!" Majesta said. She was spreading glittery lotion across her chest. She was rocking a black tube dress, pointy red Versace heels, and a red Versace bag to match.

"I don't know. From what I hear, he likes her a lot," my sister announced as she applied mascara to her eyelashes. "He has her truck all the time. Her uncle offered him a job at his bakery. Plus, I heard they were at Chuck E. Cheese's the other day, eating like one big, happy family."

I brushed my teeth as I listened to my sister and Majesta argue for a bit. When I was done, I sat on the lid of my toilet seat and put on my green Converse to go with the outfit I had on.

"Well, Corey has a girl. I got Bobbie, so who cares?" I stated, putting an end to their argument.

I straightened my sister's hair and then gave her two French braids that went down the sides of her neck.

When we all emerged from the bathroom, Bruce and Bobbie were already taking shots of whiskey. People from around the neighborhood were at the house as well. We all drank shots and then took group pictures. After we were done, we all left for the club.

Club Shady was right around the corner from the house, but we still drove over there. By the time we got there, a long line had formed outside the front door.

People from the other two clubs in the area, clubs that had closed thirty minutes ago, were waiting to get inside. As we stood outside waiting our turn to go through the doors, we joked around with each other and laughed.

About fifteen minutes after we got in line, I caught a glimpse of an electric-blue Chevy Tahoe, which had pulled into the parking lot. It had twenty-six-inch rims on it and tinted windows. I watched as Corey hopped out on the driver's side. He was fresh to death in his neatly starched Robin's jeans. Dollie climbed out on the passenger side and pulled open a hidden door so Young Soljah, a homie from the neighborhood, could get out. I had to admit, Dollie was working that navy-blue Prada dress with the matching heels. Her hair was done in a neat updo, with ringlets cascading down and around her face.

Young Soljah was older than me and was a goon, for real. He loved jacking people, and anything you wanted, he could get for you. He was tall and dark skinned, and he resembled a roadrunner to me, especially with the uncombed 'fro he was trying to grow. From a distance, you could see clear as day that he hadn't combed it, which threw his Coogi outfit off. You had to be on point from head to toe, and Young Soljah never was. That was my nigga, though, with his scrawny black ass.

I watched as Dollie grabbed Corey's hand. The three of them walked up to the front of the line and disappeared inside.

"What the hell did she just do?" I heard Majesta say.

Dollie had bypassed everybody in line like she was Queen Bee or something.

"She thinks she gets red-carpet treatment," said a black girl behind us.

I felt my heart drop at that moment, since we had been waiting in the line for over twenty minutes, and it was moving at a crawl. As it turned out, we waited another fifteen minutes before we could finally get inside.

Once we stepped foot inside the club, it was packed. Bobbie grabbed my hand so we wouldn't lose each other. I grabbed Majesta's hand so she wouldn't lose us, either. Bruce located my brother Drew.

Bruce, my brother-in-law, was tall and dark. He was made of nothing but muscle and was very quiet, like my brother. He was actually my brother's best friend. He was the only one in our hood whom Drew trusted, and they had been aces since they were nine years old. Bruce was far from handsome, but his thuggish ways and his ride-or-die loyalty had made every hood chick want the nigga. They were sick when they found out he had married my sister.

Drew was holding tables for us that were right by the pool tables. He gave my sister and me a hug. Then Majesta pulled out a throwaway camera, and we began taking pictures again.

"Don't forget about ya boy!" Corey said as he approached us with several of the homies in tow. He had a Black & Mild in his mouth and was holding a Budweiser.

Corey positioned himself between Bruce and Drew. We all jumped in the picture while my friend snapped away.

"Where's your bitch at?" Majesta teased him after we were through taking pictures.

Corey took his Black out of his mouth and looked at her. "Her name is Dollie, and she's out there dancing."

That answer shut Majesta up. She tried to recover by attempting to change the subject, but Corey brushed her off. Justine looked over at me, and I just shook my head.

As the night wore on, I forgot about Corey, as the whiskey shots from earlier had started to kick in. Some of the big homies got me some Crown Royal and Coke.

I was faded. Majesta and I walked around the club and started chatting with people that we knew. I decided to head over to the bar to get one of the big homies to get me a Long Island Iced Tea.

"How you been, li'l mama?" I heard a voice whisper in my ear.

I turned and looked up to see Corey right behind me. "What's up, stranger?" I said to him. I couldn't even lie. I was happy he was speaking to me.

"Trying to lay low and stay out of trouble. You and Bobbie still together?" he said, nodding his head in the direction of the pool table where Bobbie and Drew were involved in a game.

I sighed and nodded my head.

"When you ready for a change, holla at ya boy!" he said with a huge smile on his face.

"Are *you* ready for a change?" I challenged him.

He threw me another smile before he walked off.

Let the games begin!

Chapter 8

The next couple of days were pretty busy for me with the kids. Tyrese had a cold. Hanson had gotten bitten by a spider while he was with Bobbie's parents. So that Monday, I dropped my baby daddy off at work so I could use the car and take the kids to see the doctor. Then on Tuesday, Karen caught Tyrese's cold, so my sister took her to the doctor for me. I decided to wash all the kids' sheets and thoroughly clean their rooms. I also decided to have the youngest two share a room since they were sick. Marie was going to sleep in Hanson's room until Tyrese and Karen were both feeling better.

That Wednesday, I was able to get Majesta to come over and watch my kids. I had to go pay bills. My mom came and picked me up so I could use her boyfriend's truck. After I paid the electricity bill, I headed over to Top Nails to get my nails redone and a new pedicure.

After I was through there, I headed over to my brother, Drew's house to say what's up. As I pulled up, I noticed that Koa's red Focus was in Drew's parking spot and Corey's girlfriend's truck was in the parking spot beside it. I pulled up on the other side of Koa's car. I checked myself out in the mirror, wishing I had done more with my hair than wear it back in a bun.

I opened the truck door, and before I shut it, I checked myself out one last time. I pulled my black tank top over my belly and smoothed my jeans down. I made sure that my neatly pedicured toes hadn't smudged. I slid my

Deréon shades on and closed the door. I headed up the stairs to Drew's apartment and knocked on the door.

My little brother was doing all right for himself. He hustled, and his girl had a regular job at a telemarketing company. They were living in a little one-bedroom apartment that could easily be a two- bedroom due to the study the apartment came with. It was perfect for him and Koa.

"What's up, Ten?" Drew said as he threw open the door.

I gave my little brother a hug and walked over to sit on his couch. Just then, Corey emerged from the bathroom. He looked so fine in his black tee. His pants were creased, and he had on a black pair of Jordans. He must have noticed I was staring at him, because he laughed at me.

"How I look, Ten?" Corey joked as he sat down.

I laughed at him. "You look a'ight. What you got planned today?" I coyly replied as I positioned my body toward him.

He shrugged his shoulders.

Drew took a seat on the couch, and he and Corey began to reminisce about the past. We all talked for about thirty minutes, until it was time for Drew to pick Koa up from work. He let us know we could kick it there until he got back from getting his girl.

Corey was rolling up his sweet by then. "All right, son," he responded, distracted by what he was doing.

When Drew closed the door, Corey began to speak to me. "Sorry I didn't get at ya right away. My mom and them came down. Plus, I've been busy with my girl."

"I ain't mad, but damn, you could have said hi," I commented.

He passed me the blunt after he took a hit.

"You right. What's up with Bobbie?" he asked as he leaned back.

We continued our conversation while smoking the blunt together.

"I don't have to pick up my girl until five. Let me get some of that," he said when the blunt was finished.

I was fucked up. I gazed hard at his finger as he pointed in between my legs. I ain't even going to lie. I hesitated a little, because I knew if I took it there with him, something good or bad would eventually happen. But I'd been hungry for attention, thirsty to be loved, and I knew this was just sex, not love. I wasn't worried at all about Bobbie. Evidently, he wasn't worried about his bitch, either.

"Come on and hurry up, before my brother gets back," I said.

Chapter 9

Corey and I continued to see each other on a regular basis. He'd come over to my house while Bobbie was at work. Sometimes, I'd leave the house as soon as Bobbie came home. He didn't seem to care whether I stayed or left. We were growing further and further apart.

Obviously, Corey didn't feel too much for his girl, either. He was coming to my house, driving her shit. If you didn't respect your girl, you couldn't love her, so obviously, he didn't love her. But he did try to hide me from the bitch.

The neighborhood was throwing a birthday bash for Corey at the pool hall. Of course, we all made sure that word didn't get to Bobbie, so he wouldn't be tempted to go. Justine came to pick me up. I had decided not to overdo it while getting ready, or Bobbie would have really peeped game on the scene.

I had also made sure to cook a big dinner, big enough to shut Bobbie's ass up. As a matter of fact, I'd gone as far as to make sure it was done before he got home. I had even picked up the house. I didn't want shit to look too obvious, so I had left some shit out here and there. Then I took off with Justine, and we headed to the pool hall.

The pool hall was located in the same run-down building that Club Shady was in. The inside of the pool hall wasn't really much. The floors were cement, and you could tell where there used to be carpet on them, because some of the old glue was still there. The windows were dirty, as were the glass doors. The men's and women's bathrooms were big enough for six people each, give or take, but each one had only two stalls.

The whole main area of the pool hall was bright, and they had eight pool tables up front. There was a dance floor to the left, and on the other side of that dance floor were eight more pool tables. Leather couches lined the walls behind those pool tables, and they looked like they had been cut up. So, of course, if you were wearing shorts, a dress, or a skirt, you couldn't sit on them, unless you wanted the leather to cut your skin.

The bar sat on the right side of the first set of pool tables. It was long, and normally, only two people would be behind it. You could tell the bar was the only thing the owner of the pool hall really cared about, because the countertop was granite and the rest of the bar was refurbished and painted black. Behind the bar was a big-ass see-through fridge that took up the entire length of the wall. You could see what kind of beer, wine, and liquor they had in there.

"Drew and Corey are already there. Corey and his girl are arguing, so he ain't in her truck," Justine said as we drove away from my house.

"Oh. Well, I'll take care of him," I joked.

My heart raced as we pulled up into the parking lot. I could see that some of our Mafia homies were already inside. When we entered the building, I heard Corey shout out to me.

"Baby!" he yelled, drawing out every syllable as he spoke. He was running up to me while holding a cigar in his hand. He gave me a big hug and then walked around with me, his arm wrapped around my waist. "You're gonna be my girl. You need to tell Bobbie to move around, 'cause Daddy's moving in."

I looked at him and smiled. I was a little shocked at what he had just said. On the cool, I was ready for Bobbie to move out, and I did want Corey to move in. I was just surprised he had said it like that. I stayed glued to his side for the majority of the night. When Justine was ready to leave, Corey kissed me good-bye.

After Justine and I got in her car, we headed to Whataburger to get something to eat. While we waited in the drive-through, I told Justine about the comment Corey had made.

"Wow, big sis! What are you going to do?"

"I think I want Bobbie to leave. I don't love him anymore. We don't talk to each other anymore. I love how Corey makes me feel," I said to my sister.

"Corey's selling dope again. That's why him and Dollie are fighting. She seems pretty cool, but she's too good for him," Justine replied.

"I don't care what's going on between the two of them. I just care about me and him. Who gives a fuck about Corey and Dollie?" I retorted.

By now we had made it to the cashier. We paid for our food, grabbed the bags, and headed to my house.

"You better look for a job. If Bobbie leaves, your bill money leaves too," Justine warned.

"I'll have him pay child support. I'll get food stamps. I'm already on HUD. I'll be all right."

What the hell was up with Justine? I thought to myself.

"Just be careful with him. Corey's cool, but I've heard stories about him. Make sure you are doing the right thing, 'cause you have four little ones to think about as well," Justine said.

I nodded my head.

Justine dropped me off, rather than staying and sharing a burger with me. Instead of going inside my house, I sat on my front porch and ate my food. After I ate my last french fry, I rested my head on my hands. *How do I make Bobbie leave? Do I want him to go, or do I want him to stay? The children are attached to him. Shit. That's their daddy*, I mused. I gazed off into space as I thought about it some more. When I got up, I had made up my mind.

My baby daddy was going to have to leave, and that was all there was to it.

Chapter 10

Dollie

"Baby, I'll be there around one thirty to pick you up for lunch. I'm running behind and got something to do," my boyfriend told me from the other end of the phone.

"That's cool, babe," I said. I told him I loved him before I hung up the phone.

Ever since my man had got out, I had had nothing but smiles on my face. He was a true prince, and I loved being with him. I had started letting him use the truck during the day. He had meetings to attend as part of the terms of his parole, and he also was trying to get his ID and his Social Security card straightened out. Of course, all that had vanished when he got locked up, but he had to have that in order to get a job. I sure was glad he was on top of things. It had been a week and a half since he got out, and he was doing amazingly well.

Applause coming from the doorway brought me back to the reality of work. I jerked my head up to see who was clapping their hands. My coworker Tammy stood in the doorway. I burst out laughing at her. She, on the other hand, had a little attitude.

"You're in la-la land, lady!" She walked over to her desk and rested her brand-new Luis Vuitton briefcase on her desk. "That was your little convict, huh?"

I rolled my eyes at her comment. It wasn't a surprise to me that she disliked him. I loved Tammy, but I hated when her energy changed once the conversation concerned him. However, I was in the relationship with him, not her. I dealt with him, not her. She just wasn't meant to understand. As long as I got it, that was all that really counted. Nobody could disrupt the smile fastened to my face.

I had to confess, I was more in love with him now than I had been before. Plus, the sex was ten times better than I remembered. His voice made my heart melt every time he called me baby. I'm telling you, this boy had my mind gone.

I had worn my hair down that day. I'd curled my hair so that big curls fell past my shoulders. The curls kept getting in my eyes. I didn't mind. I felt as beautiful and loved on the outside as I did internally.

"He was just telephoning to let me know he'll be here at one thirty," I replied.

Tammy stood behind her desk and looked dramatically at her watch. I smiled to myself at her exaggerated entertainment. I leaned back to see what she was going to say next. I had no idea why she refused to give Corey a chance. If she got to know him, she would like him a lot. Especially now.

"That's another hour and a half from now. What you gonna do until then?" She sat in her chair and opened her briefcase.

Tammy had just come back from meeting with a promising new consumer in Baird for Jerry. He couldn't make it, since he was going to be in court in San Angelo all day. I could see that she was getting ready to type up the file for Jerry so he could evaluate it later.

"I've done almost everything except type up these last payment notices," I informed her. "I was saving these for after lunch, but I'll go on ahead and do them now."

I pulled out the list that Jerry had given me so I could get started. We both worked in silence for thirty minutes, both of us taking turns answering the phone.

Tammy had to remain in the office to talk to patrons in jail. They were supposed to begin calling around two o'clock, and she was going to be busy talking to them from two to four. Then, at four thirty, she had to go meet with another potential client in Tye. I knew this was going to be one of those days when she would be working after hours. I wasn't too concerned about it.

At the end of our thirty minutes of silence, Tammy pushed herself away from her desk and came and sat in the chair in front of mine. She waited silently for me to look up and begin chatting with her. I was too preoccupied and was on a roll with my task. I was determined to finish before my man arrived.

"So?" she finally said.

Her red hair was flatironed straight, which showed off it lusciousness and thick dimensions. Her white Gucci suit made her mane stand out, and her electric-blue eyes mesmerized you behind her Dolce & Gabbana glasses.

I snickered at her. I made her wait as I finished typing out my fifth notice letter. Then I hit PRINT on the computer screen and made her wait some more while I left to retrieve the letter. I sat down at my desk and placed the letter in its proper envelope. I forced myself away from the keyboard to face her. She now had my undivided attention.

"All is good. Ten times better than before," I said, giving her the lowdown.

"Is that so?" She took a piece of my Doublemint gum and unwrapped it. She eyed me.

I filled her in on everything that was going on, from the plans to move to Bedford to him always being here with me lately. It was like he had done a complete one-eighty.

Maybe my baby getting locked up was what he had needed, after all.

"You guys ain't together twenty-four-seven, right?"

"Of course not." I tittered to myself. "I just feel like we are making up for lost time."

"I wish you the best, though." I didn't trust that tone in her speech. It didn't match the expression on her face. She had turned serious on me quick, and I could feel the caution in her voice. Her sincerity was spreading over her face.

I hated to admit it, but I could feel bad vibes rush through my body, and then there was a tug at my heart at that very moment. *A woman's intuition? About what?* Something was not right at this moment. I didn't know exactly what it was. How could something go wrong at this moment when everything was going fine right now? Just as fast as that hunch came over me, I shrugged it off.

I could tell that Tammy wanted to say more, so I leaned toward her to let her know I was listening. She was my friend, and her opinion did really matter to me. However, I just knew I had to use my very own discernment as much as I could.

"Love makes us all do crazy things, girl. Has you thinking a piece of shit on the concrete is fresh, beautiful red roses. Don't let him fool you and get you down, Dollie. Don't believe the hype. Remember actions speaks louder than words. Before you go anywhere with him—I mean, up and move out of Abilene—you make sure he ain't bullshittin' you first. I just don't trust that man at all."

Chapter 11

It had been a couple of days since my last encounter with Tammy. I knew her schedule was going to be busy. Jerry had to be in court in San Angelo every day that week, which meant Tammy had to do his interviews for him. However, today she wasn't interviewing. She actually had to go to San Angelo to help Jerry defend two of his clients. So I knew I wasn't going to see either one of them today.

Tammy's words had never left me. But they didn't get me down. After all, she wasn't with Corey. I was. I had let him use my truck again. We had spent the night at his grandma's house, just talking and laughing with each other. We couldn't say that it was like old times. Not at all. It was more like something new, something I had never done with him. I had to admit, I was hooked on him.

I had worn something simple to work today. I had put on a pair of nice jeans and a black short-sleeved shirt. I had neatly combed my long hair into an updo, and a big gray banana clip was holding it up. I had on a pair of black heels and my black hoop earrings. I was modestly dressed but stunning at the same time.

My son had stayed up with us until bedtime last night. Even though we were at Corey's grandma's house, Drake had wanted to sleep in his own bed. So, we had to take him home. My aunt and uncle had agreed to look after him that night.

Corey had dropped me off at work this morning, promising to pick me up for lunch. We had decided that we'd pick up Drake and take him to McDonald's during my lunch break. I knew my son would like that.

This morning the office was busy. I had clients pouring in to drop off payments. I was also getting data from new clients and setting up meeting times. Old clients were calling, wanting updates and information about their pending cases. I knew it was going to be a while before they spoke directly to Jerry. His schedule was full. He was going to be in court in San Angelo, Sweetwater, and Big Spring over the next three weeks, so a lot of the client meetings had to wait until after that. And if any of the hearings were delayed, it would be anywhere from three weeks to a month before Jerry was available. The best way clients had to contact him was speaking with his paralegal. So unless they agreed to meet with Tammy, it was going to be a minute before they talked with him.

The first thing on my agenda after handling the clients was to run to the bank to deposit money. So as soon I got the chance, which meant as soon as the office was clear, I opened the safe, took out the cash and checks, and then I bolted down the block to the bank. While I treasured the times when the office was busy, since it made my time at work go by so much faster, today's pace had been a little too frenetic.

When Corey arrived to pick me up for lunch, I was scheduling a meeting with a long-standing client for Tammy. Corey and Bruce both walked into the office, but I was so busy, I didn't notice them at first. They were watching me talk and type at the same time. As soon as I hung up the phone, Corey spoke. I swiftly raised my head up, with a huge grin on my face.

"Damn. Look at my baby typing all fast and shit," he joked.

I laughed at him and flashed him a smile, revealing my perfect pearly whites. Bruce was a very good friend of Corey's. He was married to a very beautiful young woman named Justine. She was Drew's older sister. I had come to know her while Corey was locked up. We weren't best friends or anything, but she was a cool female. She was always with Bruce when I ran into them over at the bakery. Bruce always gave me some money to put on my man's books or some message he wanted me to deliver to him.

Bruce was tall and dark. He was somewhat discreet, but he had a mean streak to him. He rode for anybody who was from his neighborhood, which was dumb to me. But I didn't understand that or him, so I could care less about that lifestyle. To me, he was satisfactory, but I also sensed that he was a corrupting influence on Corey. He sold drugs. Well, really, a lot of them did. People said he was a snitch, and that was why everybody but him always seemed to get caught up. How true that was, I would never know.

Corey informed me that we were taking Bruce to go get his car from the house of his sister-in-law, who was Drew's sister. I guessed that Drew had another sister. I never seen that one before. I had just always assumed that it was just him and Justine.

We ended up dropping Bruce off around the corner, at the store. Bruce said he'd walk the rest of the way to get his car. For a second, I found that suspicious. After leaving Bruce, Corey took me by the day care to pick up Drake. On the way there, I questioned Corey about Bruce's actions.

"What's up with that stunt at the store?"

He took a moment to answer. "What stunt, Doll?"

"You told me that we needed to go take him to his sister-in-law's. Why did we drop him off at the store, and not at her house?"

"Man, her old man be tripping. He act funny when people he don't know pull up at their house and shit. That's why."

I accepted that answer, and the rest of the way to the day care, I listened to that new Z-Ro album, *Drankin' & Drivin'*. We pulled up to the spot, and we both got out. While I signed my son out, Corey talked with my aunt Audrina in her office. I had primed my aunt, letting her know that he would be returning. Before we left, she hugged each of us and said that taking Drake was fine.

"Bring me back a burger, Drake!" she teased him.

"Okay, Aunt Drina," he shouted back as he ran ahead of us to wait for Corey and me to catch up to him at the front door.

I drove to McDonald's, since Drake wanted to sit in Corey's lap. Normally, I would have made him get in his car seat, but today I didn't. I loved that Drake liked Corey. I loved more that Corey liked my son back. Their bond was quite unique. It made me love the man even more.

We made it to McDonald's and ordered our food. We all ate in the play area. After Drake was done, he went to play in the balls with two other little boys, whose parents were nearby. Corey gave his undivided attention to me. We talked for a minute before he broke the news to me.

"My grandpa is sick. I need to go see him. His birthday is this weekend. My mom and them are throwing him a party in Denton. Her and her sisters have been working on it and invited us to come down."

"Oh, that sounds fun. Drake also?"

"Man, hell, yeah! That's my son too. Hell you mean?"

I was beaming from the way he said that.

"So we going down there?" he asked.

"Yeah, I'm down, my love," I said, biting into one of my fries.

"Good, 'cause I already told them we would be there," he confessed.

"Okay, baby. That's what's up." I giggled at his goofy ass. He let me know that we were going to leave that Friday and would come back Sunday. He also informed me that we were going to stay at his mama's house in Bedford. We lingered at McDonald's for another twenty minutes to finish up our food and go over our weekend plans. Afterward, Corey dropped me off at work first and then drove off to take my son back to the day care.

Chapter 12

The rest of the week flew by in a blur. Work being so busy here lately, along with shopping and preparing myself for the trip, contributed to time flying by. That Friday, my day at my job went by like crazy, just as I had predicted, judging by how every day at work had been pretty busy that week. Sure enough, five o' clock arrived right on time, and Corey was outside in the truck, waiting on me, with Drake in the backseat. He already had his big cookie from my uncle Justin's bakery.

Corey had our bags in the bed of the truck, covered up by my bedsheets. I got in the truck, and we headed toward the highway. Corey was rapping to that new Ro album. The album had barely just dropped, and he already knew by heart all the words to every song. He loved him some Ro.

"We gonna stay at my mom's tonight and then go meet up with everybody else for a big family get-together in Denton tomorrow, It's a party for my grandpa," he reported.

I knew he couldn't wait to see his grandpa. His grandma had died years ago, and when she passed, he'd been locked up. I knew it meant everything to him to be around while his grandpa, at least, could see him.

By the time we pulled up to his mom's house, Drake was sound asleep. Me, I was almost dead to the world too. I woke up just as we pulled into his mom's driveway.

Corey's mom had a small two-story ranch-style home. It was white, and there were big windows all over the house. Her front yard was large, and I could tell her grass was fake by the color of it. She had dandelions in her garden in front of her large porch. She had a big white fence along the back of her house, and I could tell she had a huge backyard as well.

A chaotic scene greeted us. Corey had spoken with his mom while we were on the road, and she had told him what was up. From what I could tell by what Corey was saying, Tiger was here and his mom was mad. Naomi was supposed to pick up her daughter after she got off from work, but she hadn't come to get her yet. What was new? I just shook my head in disbelief.

Corey's mom was on the porch, crying, and Tiger was on his cell phone, yelling at the top of his lungs. It sounded like he was yelling at his sister. Or at least one might have guessed that was the case, since she was the one causing the problems at the moment. Naomi's little girl, Nestle, was observing what was going on.

"Man, I'm going to whup Naomi's ass, 'cause she know better than that," Corey muttered out loud to himself as he turned the engine off.

Corey got out of the truck and headed toward Tiger. He took the phone out of his hand and spoke to his sister. "Bring yo' mothafuckin' ass over here before I fuck you up, Naomi! Grow the fuck up and quit actin' like a ho," he barked, arguing with her as well.

In the midst of this, Tiger approached me and spoke apologetically. "I am so sorry about this. This isn't the way I wanted you to see us."

"No. That's okay. Everybody has family problems," I assured him.

I took my sleepy son out of his car seat and into the house, and Tiger showed me the way to the bedroom we were going to be sleeping in. As I passed by his mom, she greeted me. I could tell she was extremely upset by the way she was shaking. When we reached the bedroom, I laid my son in the middle of the bed and sat on the edge of it.

Moments later, Tiger and Corey were carrying our luggage into the bedroom. His mom followed behind. Her face was red and blotchy from crying. She cracked a smile and motioned for me to come and give her a hug.

"Nice to meet you, Doll. I am so sorry," she said to me as we hugged.

"No. It's okay."

The sadness that filled her eyes made me want to reach in and pull it out. I didn't totally understand her pain, what she battled with on a daily basis as far as her children were concerned. I knew enough about motherhood to tell that she tried her hardest to do her very best.

"Don't be sad. Be happy we made it!" I said, trying to cheer her up with some positive words.

"Honey, if it ain't one thing, it's another." She hugged me again very tightly.

When his mom walked out of the bedroom, Corey followed behind her, trying to get the scoop on what was going on. I took one of my bags into the bathroom and took a nice long bath. When I was done, I walked back into the bedroom and immediately noticed that my son wasn't there. I figured Corey had him and went to greet them all. Corey had gotten his mom to calm down. Drake and Nestle were sitting on the living-room floor, playing with one of his trucks. I went over to the couch and took a seat beside Corey. Tiger had already left, with the promise that he'd be in Denton after he was done coaching his Little League game in the morning.

"I swear, your sister is the most selfish, ungrateful little bitch ever," his mom said. She was sitting in the recliner, covered up by a checkered blanket.

Her face had begun to clear up, but her eyes were still bloodshot from all the crying she had done. She was smoking a cigarette to help her calm down. Corey placed his arm around me and twirled my hair with his finger as he focused his attention on his mom.

"As soon as she walks through the door, I'm gonna beat her ass," he declared.

"Corey—" his mom began, but he cut her off.

"Fuck that. I didn't come down here to babysit. You ain't volunteered to babysit. Tiger didn't, and my wife ain't babysitting, either." His voice was filled with anger. "If she didn't want a baby, she should have kept her damn legs closed."

Brenda, Corey's mom, tried to calm him down. The more she tried, the more annoyed he became. So after thirty minutes, she gave up and went to bed. It was going on eleven, and Naomi still hadn't shown up. I had just laid my son down to sleep when I heard a loud popping sound. I left the bedroom and quickly closed the door on my way out, hoping that the commotion wouldn't wake my son up.

I ran down the stairs. I entered the living room to witness Corey pinning his drunken little sister down on the floor. She was screaming for help, but I couldn't move. Well, truthfully, I wasn't going to help her. I secretly hoped Corey would knock some common sense into that girl. Right then, Brenda came out of her bedroom and ran past me. Instead of helping Corey, she slapped Naomi in her face. She was like a raging bull. Her target was her only daughter.

"You are one sorry motherfucker! How fuckin' evil are you, Naomi! And you're drunk too? Ooh, fuckin' stink! No way is Nestle walking out of this house with your ass. Fuck that. You're leaving my granddaughter here!"

"You ain't leaving here with my niece," Corey said, chiming in.

Naomi stood up and tried so hard to stay in one place. It was quite an amusing sight to see. This pretty woman slurring every word, trash faced, and leaning from side to side, lookin' like a fish that had just got caught on somebody's line. Well, Corey's line, anyway.

"Fuck you. Fuck both of y'all. I'm still young. I can have fun," Naomi said incoherently.

Corey cocked his hand back and slapped the fire out of Naomi. He whacked her so hard, she fell backward on the floor and rolled over in perfect somersault. He reached in her pockets and took her car keys. She tried unsuccessfully to stop him. He looked at his mom.

"She's staying here. I dare her to take these keys from me. I'll beat her ass first. She better get some act right, Mom. I'm back, and I'll beat the brakes off her ass, for real."

"She can stay here, but she's sleeping on the porch," his mom said.

She opened the front door and told Naomi to leave. Naomi stumbled toward her mom, as if she was fixing to hit her. That was enough to set Corey off again. He pushed her so hard out the front door that she landed right dead on her face on the front porch. My mouth dropped as I observed this scene before me. Corey walked back in the house, slammed the door behind him, and locked it.

"Let her try to sneak off this property by driving one of these cars. I'll beat the brakes off her ass too. Real talk," he snarled.

Chapter 13

The next day went by smoothly. It was as if last night had never even happened. I had no idea what to think about how fast everybody had forgotten about the drunken mess. Naomi apologized to Corey and her mom that morning, the first chance she got. She even called Tiger at home and told him she was sorry. You could tell there had been a scuffle. Naomi had a nice bruise forming on her left cheek. Her forehead had a scrape on it from her landing on the front porch the way she had. I was positive she was going to try to get in her brother's face. Corey was expecting it too, but she didn't.

Naomi had to run to her apartment to get ready for the big family gathering that was being held in Denton, so we agreed to bring Nestle with us. We all decided to ride together. We were going to take my ride, and Brenda was going to drive, since she knew exactly where in Denton we were headed and how to get there. Our first stop was the nursing home where Corey's grandfather lived. We arrived there at the exact same time that Brenda's two younger sisters pulled up in a van.

Evangeline was the middle child. She wasn't married but had a son who was going to school at Harvard. Naomi had described her to me as really snobby and selfish. She had red hair too. She was a little on the heavy side and reminded me of those stuck-up white ladies you would see on TV. The ones who carried their little dogs in a purse. She spoke properly, so you could tell she was well educated. She even did everything in a very proper manner.

"Corey! How are you?" Evangeline walked up to him with her arms out. Corey hugged her and gave her a kiss. I watched as she made a big fuss over him. Any attention my man got, he always ate up. Especially if it was a female who was praising him for being so fine or expressing how proud she was to have him as family. At least this was a blood family. Not no "fake" homegirls trying to claim him as family, and he already fucked.

The other sister was built more like Brenda. She wore her hair short and curly. She had on some sunshades and carried a purse you'd see in the dollar store. I was told this sister was the loaded one. She was a dentist, and her husband owned a franchise of Wendy's restaurants around the Dallas area. They didn't have any kids. Her name was Priscilla, and she seemed very nice and down to earth. Naomi had warned me she was bipolar and sometimes would forget to take her medicine. She also said that Priscilla had tried to kill herself several times, but when she stuck to her medicine, she was fine.

"Hey, handsome," she cooed at Corey after he let go of Evangeline.

"What's up, Aunt Prissy!"

He hugged and kissed her too. Then he introduced my son and me to his aunts. We stood outside in the parking lot of the nursing home and chatted for a while. His two aunts asked me question after question. Nothing embarrassing, just a genuine interrogation. It was obvious to me that they were mostly wondering how tight my head was on my shoulders.

Brenda and Evangeline eventually headed inside to check on their dad. When they brought him outside, Corey raced over and hugged him and spoke with him for a while. It was cute watching him and his grandpa tease each other and cackle. Then Corey helped his two aunts load his grandpa into Evangeline's van. His two aunts then climbed in.

Everyone riding in my truck hopped back in, and we followed Evangeline's van to the hotel where they had reserved a banquet room. That was where they were having the party. When we got there, Corey helped his aunt Evangeline get his grandpa out of the van. I helped Priscilla bring in the food and arrange it nicely on the table in the banquet room. Then we organized the chairs. Brenda watched over the kids while we set up.

Naomi arrived soon after Corey wheeled his granddad into the banquet room. More of the family members began to show up in rapid succession after that. Corey was making it a point to introduce his girlfriend who worked at the lawyer's office. Tiger arrived an hour later with his family. They were the last ones everybody was waiting for. The party began.

The rest of the afternoon was quite fun. Corey's mom and his aunts had put together quite an action-packed day. We all played the games that his grandpa loved. Then everybody shared inspirational stories about his grandpa and his grandpa's late wife. Corey's grandfather even told some stories. The cake they had selected for his party was rather beautiful. It was a five-layer chocolate cake with red roses going all the way around it.

The party lasted until six thirty. When it was over, we all said our good-byes, and then Tiger and Corey helped load their granddad into Evangeline's van. Tiger and his family then followed the van back to the nursing home. Naomi took the very sleepy children back to her mom's house in Bedford. Brenda and I straightened up the banquet room, and then Brenda drove Corey and me back to Bedford.

Once we were inside the house, I left Brenda, Corey, and Naomi alone so I could check on my son. I took a hot shower before I went back to the living room. When I walked in, I immediately sensed something was wrong. Corey was outside, talking to Naomi in her car. Brenda was sitting on the couch, looking disgusted.

"What's up?" I asked her.

"You tell me," she said.

A wave of confusion spread through me. Feeling myself getting defensive, I folded my arms across my chest and sized up Corey's mom. I didn't know what to say at first, so I chose my words carefully before I spoke.

"No, you tell me what's going on. I'm not a mind reader."

Corey's grandma had warned me about Ms. Brenda before. She had told me that his mom's side kept a lot of shit up. I really was starting to see that now, especially after the bullshit that had happened last night. These white people over here were all the way about bullshit.

She puffed on her cigarette before she placed it in the ashtray. She looked up at me. I could tell she was pissed. "According to my daughter, you've been cheating on my son."

I burst out laughing. Who the fuck was Naomi? She didn't even fuck with nobody in Abilene, so for her to fix her mouth and say some bullshit like that was messy as hell.

"She claims to have proof."

I shook my head. "Well, where is this proof? If anything, you two should recognize that I was there for Corey the entire time. I need to see this proof."

Chapter 14

Tenosha

The conversation I had with Corey had never once left my mind. It had been a few days since I'd seen him, but I was determined to get Bobbie out of here. I had decided to just do me. Bobbie and I weren't in love with each other anymore. We just stayed together for the kids. The real question was, how the hell was I going to pull this off? No way I was about to leave. I was the one who had the kids, so it was only right that I keep the house. He could go move back in with his parents.

That day, Bobbie let me keep the car so I could run errands. I decided to go on ahead and file so that his ass had to pay child support. I didn't want to work and wasn't really looking forward to seeking work. But, shit, if I had to clock in at somebody's business to make ends meet on my own, then so be it. Bobbie had to go. His time was up.

He was a damn good father. Don't get me wrong. And, really, the truth was, he didn't deserve to be forced to pay child support, because he did do for the kids. I had to give that fool that much: he did right when it came to those kids. But as far as "us" went, it was over. We were done. So, he had to go, and the only way to keep money flowing in my house until I was able to get a job was to put them white folks in his life. At least that would take care of the bills.

I had to pick up Majesta so she could help me with the kids while I was out. Ty and Karen could be a handful at times, but I wasn't concerned. I knew those two acted right when Majesta was around. They loved her so much.

"Hey, Majesta," I greeted as I pulled up in front of her granny's house.

"Hey, lady," she said, sliding into the passenger seat. "Love your hair. It's sexy."

I smiled at Majesta. I had decided to straighten my hair that morning. I had pulled it all up into a very cute ponytail.

Majesta glanced back and smiled at Tyrese and Karen in the backseat as I pulled away from the house. I headed out of the neighborhood and drove in the direction of the attorney general's office, where I planned to file for child support. On the way I listened to T.I. over the car speakers. Majesta and the two little ones conversed with each other for a little bit. Then she turned her attention back to me.

"So, guess what the word is," she said eagerly to me.

"Tell me."

"Corey's hot girl cheated on him the entire time he was locked up. That bitch is so stupid."

"Bitch! How you know?"

"Corey called me and told me what was going on. Some shit Naomi told him. And, of course, who you gonna believe? Your sister or that bitch?"

"Your fucking sister!" I said.

"Exactly."

I couldn't believe my ears. I hadn't seen this shit coming at all. I had thought I was going to have to put a little work into it. I knew Corey felt some type of way about that girl, but real shit, that was bananas. His perfect woman wasn't so perfect, after all. She was just a trashy bitch with a good job and a fuckin' truck. She didn't even have her own house. Yeah, she was perfect, all right. The main thing was that this made Corey fair game, and, anyway, he was cheating on her with me. I was in the door and had him right where I wanted him.

"She is stupid," I said. "Now I don't feel bad anymore for fuckin' with him."

"Bitch, I knew it!" my best friend screamed.

I told Majesta about my plan to put Bobbie out and, hopefully, to have Corey move in. That was one thing I could say. At least I had my own place. That dumb-ass bitch didn't. That Goody Two-shoes still lived with somebody else, like a little kid, and she was way older than me too. *Bitch, please.*

"How are you gonna kick Bobbie out? That would be fucked up, but Corey is fine as hell. You better get that nigga."

"Oh, I got him. I'm already claiming it too, girl. Checkmate!" I stated assertively.

Majesta changed the CD from T.I. to E.S.G. as we chatted away about some other gossip that was going on in the neighborhood. After I pulled up to the building where the child support office was located, Majesta stayed in the car with the kids and I ran inside. I was gone for only thirty minutes. When I returned, Majesta and Tyrese, who was old enough, were eating sandwiches from Alley Cats, which was right down the street. I hopped in the car and took off back to the house. What was I going to do about Bobbie?

"Majesta, what can I do to get rid of Bobbie?" I asked my best friend. She finished chewing on her sandwich and thought for a little bit.

"You got to flip the script on him."

"But how?"

"Don't cook anymore. Don't clean. Everything he expects you to do now, stop doing it. Or just be up front and tell him you don't want him anymore. Fuck all that extra bullshit. Just tell him, 'Look you got to go.'"

She got me there. That seemed better than just playing games with him.

"How fast you want him gone?" she queried.

"By the weekend." I took a deep breath.

"Oh, you ain't wasting no time," she said.

I shook my head no.

We pulled into my driveway and got out of the car. Tyrese had made a mess with his sandwich, and I decided to leave it. I called my brother to see if he would pick up Bobbie for me, and he agreed. That right there was sure to piss Bobbie off. I also knew my family was going to be angry when they heard I had put him out. I didn't care. I knew what I wanted. And I was going to get it too.

I went and picked up Hanson and Marie from school. When I came back, I let the three older kids run around the house while Majesta and I sat outside with Karen. I knew that when Drew pulled up with Bobbie, it was going to be some shit. For one, I hadn't bothered cooking for his ass. Two, the house was a mess. And three, he'd be mad that I hadn't picked him up and instead was just sitting outside while the kids were inside, actin' a damn fool.

Sure enough, my brother pulled up in the driveway before long. Majesta and I had moved the lawn chairs underneath the shade tree. I could hear the kids inside the house, being loud as hell, so I knew they were cutting up. Bobbie didn't even acknowledge me when he got out of the car.

"Is he mad?" Majesta whispered to me.

I shrugged my shoulders. He was so hard to read these days. I hoped he was. I wanted any reason to start a fight, so the words could roll smoothly off my tongue. He needed to go.

"You stay right here, because shit's about to hit the fan," I said and clutched Majesta's hand.

She nodded at me. "I ain't missing this shit for the world, boo."

We chilled outside for another twenty minutes. When I realized Bobbie wasn't going to come outside, I decided to go in. I wanted him to argue with me. Anything so I could have an excuse to kick him out. I walked inside with my homegirl right behind me. The kids were sitting at the kitchen table, drawing. Drew and Bobbie were sitting on the couch, playing a video game.

"What the fuck?" Majesta said in my ear.

I shrugged my shoulders and sat on the recliner with Karen. Maybe it was going to be a lot tougher than I had thought. I could cause a scene, but my babies would be fucked up about it. Plus, my brother was here, and the last thing I needed was to act like an ass in front of him.

I got up and made the kids something to eat, and I purposely did not make enough for Bobbie to partake. After they were done, I left the mess on the table, and then I began to give the kids their baths. By that time, Majesta decided to go home. Drew had to go pick up his girl, and Bobbie was talking to somebody on his cell phone.

After I was done bathing the kids, I put them to bed. I walked into the living room, where Bobbie was still talking on his phone. It was now or never. I grabbed his phone from him and hung it up. I tossed it on his lap and pointed to the front door.

"We ain't working. You gotta go."

At first Bobbie looked at me. The puzzled expression on his face showed me he didn't know what I was talking about. He stared at his phone and then looked at me before looking back at his phone. I clearly saw that he was more annoyed by the fact that I had just hung up his cell phone.

"I don't want you to stay here anymore," I told him.

Bobbie grabbed the remote control and tossed it from one hand to the other. He gazed up at me. I could tell he was contemplating what he would do next. That "next" part was what I was beginning to worry about. I didn't know if he wanted to hit me or scream at me, or if he was really going to leave.

"What the fuck is wrong with you? If I leave, what the hell are you going to do? How you gonna survive without me, you dumb bitch?" he shouted. I firmly stood my ground.

"I want you to leave. It ain't working."

"You keep fucking sayin' that, but you ain't makin' any sense. That nigga got you gone right now." He turned on the TV.

Wait. What did he just say? Desperate to regain control of the conversation, I yanked the remote from his hand. I turned the TV off. I tossed the remote control behind me softly so it wouldn't break. I needed that remote control. The kids had lost the other one. A replacement cost money. And that was money I was about to not have anymore.

"Ten," he said, a warning in his voice.

"Call your mom and tell her to pick you up. I can survive by myself, but you have got to go." I picked up the remote and held on tightly to it.

"Bitch, my kids live here. How are they going to survive with you? is the real question." He sneered at me.

I had to admit that hearing him say shit like that kind of stung a little. But it was my mission to appear unbothered. I was getting a rise out of his ass, anyway. He looked like he was going to hit me. If he did, I had already prepared myself to beat his ass with the Glade air freshener can, which was within reach.

Bobbie stood up and mocked me. "Bitch, I know you heard me. The fuck you think I was? A fool? Yeah, you were running around here, acting like a ho and trying to be all secretive, like I don't know about you and Corey. That nigga ain't shit. He got you gone over dick, right?" He folded his arms across his chest and waited for me to respond. A huge-ass smirk was pasted on his face. He was getting to me, and he could see it.

"I don't know what you're talking about," I replied innocently.

"I knew you were messing around. I knew it, but I don't give a damn anymore, and I didn't give a fuck while you were fuckin' that scrub. All I care about is my kids. If you want me to go, I'll go, but I'll be damned if I allow another man to tell my kids what to do."

"I just said I don't know what you're talking about."

"Yeah, bitch, you know." He walked out of the living room and disappeared down the hall.

I was surprised that he knew my secret. As I looked at the spot where he had been standing just a second ago, something told me I was making the wrong decision. This crazy feeling that I was making a terrible choice seemed to creep all over me, especially my chest area. I shivered. Then, just like that, the feeling went away, not a trace of it left behind.

I focused my attention back on what he had just said to me. How did Bobbie know? Who had told him? Why hadn't he said anything? Saddest of all was the fact that this nigga must really not give a damn about me or what I did anymore. He just knew I was creepin' with somebody else, and he didn't even react? That was kind of fucked up, I had to admit.

I walked into the bedroom we currently shared and sat down on the bed. I watched Bobbie gather up his things. He was talking on the phone as he walked back and forth from the bedroom to the living room. I went into the living room and decided to sit on the couch. I wanted to make sure he didn't take too much shit with him when he left. I braced myself for his mother's reaction when she came to pick him up.

A half hour later, Bobbie had gathered all his things from the bedroom and was unhooking the Xbox from the TV. Right then, Bruce, Justine, and Drew walked in. Justine looked at me like I was crazy and headed toward the kids' bedrooms. Drew and Bruce talked quietly to Bobbie.

Justine came back to the front of the house and sat down on the couch in the living room. She took in the scene before her. The guys were still talking quietly and calmly, but Bobbie was clearly angry.

"Your sister lost her damn mind, bro," Bobbie told them. "She really think she fixing to maintain this house without me? I should take all this shit, 'cause I'm the reason why she has all this shit! Me! That ungrateful bitch sneaking around on me in front of my kids and shit. I hope my daughters don't grow up to be nothing like her bitch ass too!"

My sister's eyes were the size of saucers. The way my baby daddy was talking was new to her. She had rarely seen him angry before. But he was pissed now.

"Tenosha, are you crazy?" she hissed at me.

I shook my head no.

"What are you going to do?"

"Move Corey in," I whispered to her.

Just then, Drew grabbed my arm and nodded for me to follow him. When we got outside, he turned and faced me, but my attention was focused elsewhere. I was too busy looking through the window of the screen door to make sure Bobbie wasn't trying to take the flat screen.

"Are you really kicking Bobbie out to be with Corey?" Drew asked me.

"Who said that?"

"Tenosha! I just heard you tell Justine that. You acting like you was talking all quietly and shit. I heard you," he explained coolly. I just stared at him. Drew's face was covered with astonishment. The tone of his voice, however, was disgusted. "Let me tell you about Corey, Ten. That man is my nigga, and I'll ride for him, but he gotta girlfriend."

"Not for long," I said back to him.

Drew covered his face with his hand. He carefully lowered his hand and began to talk to me like I was a slow child who was hard of hearing.

"You didn't hear the news that Dollie cheated on him, huh?" I said when he was finished.

"Man, Ten, that girl didn't cheat on his ass, and if she did, oh well! That ain't your fuckin' business."

"They ain't together," I said stubbornly.

"You don't understand. He's a selfish man. He sleeps around a lot. Yeah, his ass has slowed down, Ten, but if he moves in with you, what makes you think he won't do the same thing to you that he's doing to his own girl?"

Good question, but I had a better answer.

"I ain't Dollie or any other bitch he's been with. I'm Ten. That's how I know."

My brother snorted at my response. He shook his head at me in disbelief. Right then, Bobbie came out of the house and threw some of his things into the car. I snapped. *Who the fuck that nigga thank he is, trying to take off in my car?*

"What the fuck are you doing?" I shouted as I lunged at him.

He didn't answer me. He walked by me like he didn't even notice I was there. My brother held on tightly to me. Bobbie kept loading the car up. The more shit he put in there, the harder I tried to break free from my brother. When Bobbie went back into the house, I ran to the car and began to take his shit out. Justine and Drew pulled me away and tackled me to the ground.

"Whose fuckin' side are y'all on?" I frantically tried to move but was unable to get free.

They kept me on the ground while Bobbie took his time piling his shit in the car. I was irate.

When Bobbie was done heaping his clothes up in my ride, he turned and faced me. I stopped struggling and started cursing him out as loudly as I could. I didn't give a damn who heard me or what scene I was causing. That man had me fucked up right now. I yelled until I almost lost my voice. My sister and brother never let me get up off the ground.

"This is my car. Just like if I want to come back and get everything in that fuckin' house, I will, because it belongs to me," Bobbie snarled. "This crib belongs to me. I worked for this shit, and all you did was sit on your lazy ass all fuckin' day. You had it made, bitch, but you about to learn today. You kicked me out. Therefore, I'm taking this car and all my shit with me. You figure out how to get the kids to school. You wanted this, Ten, and you got it. That nigga better not touch my fuckin' kids, or I'll kill him. If I even hear he harmed my children in any way, I'll be seeing your ass in court."

Chapter 15

The next morning, as promised, Bruce arrived to take Hanson and Marie to school. My mom and grandma were blowing up my phone like crazy. I refused to answer it, as I knew they were pissed.

I had begun to straighten up around the house. Tyrese was trying to help me. Little did he know, he was making things worse than they already were. I took a brief break, long enough to shower, get dressed, and throw my hair back into a loose ponytail. Right when I stepped out of my bedroom, I heard a knock on my door.

Who is it this time? I wondered as I walked to the front of the house. I looked out the window to see Corey standing outside. A huge smile spread across my face. I could feel myself getting all giddy inside. I let him in.

"What's up?" I asked him.

He came in and sat on the recliner. He was looking mighty delicious in his Miami Heat getup. He had on the new Nike Air Maxs that had just come out. I wrinkled my nose. That bitch had probably got them for him.

"Shit, just going through the motions. What you up to?"

I shook my head. I wanted to tell him so bad that Bobbie no longer lived here. I decided to wait until the right moment. "What you down in the dumps about?" I asked instead.

I picked up Karen and went into the kitchen. I decided to show off a little and make my kids pancakes for breakfast. Corey got up and followed me in there. He sat at the table and watched me do my thang while talking to me. Before long, Corey began to tell me about Dollie, their trip to Bedford, and how his sister claimed she was cheating on him.

So the story was true. I looked up at the ceiling and mouthed, "Thank you." I was so glad Majesta had put me up on game. I knew exactly how to play my part. Not wanting to come across like a hater, I cautiously asked him a question.

"Are you sure she was? Your sister could be throwing salt in the game. You know, causing drama."

"I ain't fucked up about it," Corey said. "You made enough for me?" Just like that he changed the subject.

He grinned at me, and I smiled back. Soon I was done burning the stove up. I had my youngest two sitting at the table and eating. I fixed Corey's plate and handed it to him.

He smiled as he took his plate and went into the living room. "Wow! I get special treatment!"

I made myself a plate and followed behind him. When we were done eating, I took his plate and mine. Then I cleared the table and washed all the dirty dishes. After I was done, I wiped down the counter and swept the kitchen floor. I wanted him to see how well I could hold down a home. Then I put Karen and Tyrese down for their nap and went into my bedroom to finish cleaning it up.

When I was halfway finished with rearranging my closet, Corey walked into my room. He sat down on my bed and looked at me with a concerned expression on his face.

"What's the matter? What's up?" I quizzed him.

"Where's the Xbox and all the games at?" He looked around my room and turned to face me. "What happened in here?"

I had dumped all my clothes out of the dresser drawers and had thrown everything on my bed. All my clothes that had been hanging in the closet were now on the floor, along with all my shoes. Clothes that I couldn't fit into were lying on top of the dresser. I was reorganizing everything to make room since the baby daddy had left.

"Looks like a damn tornado ran through here," Corey mused.

I let him rant and rave for a little while longer. I smiled to myself as I picked things up off the floor of the closet. I took a deep breath. I was going to drop the bombshell on him.

"Bobbie moved out last night," I told him nonchalantly.

Pretending to be busy, I waited for him to ask me what had happened. I guessed he was shocked by what I had just said. He didn't respond for a long time. When he finally did, I disclosed to him what had gone down. I left out the discussion I had had with my brother.

Corey's eyes widened in disbelief after I ended my story. "Damn. That was raw," he said as he lay down on the bed, He smiled at me. "Can I move in?" he said, teasing.

Or was he? I knew one thing. I wanted him more than anything. My situation with Bobbie was no longer. I needed Corey more than anything in my life. So did I want him to move in? Hell yeah! This was too easy.

"What about Dollie?" I asked innocently.

My back was turned to him on purpose. I figured if he did say that he was just playing, that he was still hung up on that bitch, I could handle that feeling of rejection better this way. I hoped he knew that he would be losing if he missed out on this bad bitch.

"Fuck that lying-ass girl, man. She's stupid. Her triflin' cheated on me," he said, then began to laugh.

Just go ahead and tell him that he can move in, a voice told me. That was what I really longed to do. A closed mouth never got fed, and occasionally, you had to take a leap of faith. Corey belonged with me. We were a much cuter match than he and that broad were. Anyway, light-skinned bitches never went out of style. So he was really winning by having me on his arm. That was when I let him know he could stay.

"Aw, for real? You want a real nigga by your side, huh?" he said.

I nodded my head. He agreed that he really wanted to move in. He got up off the bed and started helping me put my clothes up. He asked me where everything went and even told me what I should get rid of.

"Don't worry about losing any clothes, ma. I got you. I'll have you in a whole new wardrobe. You got to be on top of your game to have a nigga like me by your side."

"Boy boo! You should be the one who is glad you stepped your game up! You upgraded from playing on the C team to advancing to the A team. The fuck you mean?" I replied.

"That nigga took the car too? Let me call Doll and see if she'll let me use her truck."

I wrinkled my nose up at the sound of her name. That shit right there didn't sit too well with me. As he called her on his cell phone, I continued to straighten out my closet. Evidently, she didn't answer, because he started calling around to other people.

Corey left the room and disappeared somewhere in the front of the house. When he returned, he told me he was going around the corner to the Smiths' house. He told me that Rorie was going to take him to get his things from his grandma's.

Rorie was a square type of nigga. He was tall, scrawny. And he was a mixed breed young nigga who wanted to be down so bad. He was willing to do anything to hang with Tre. So he was pretty much the crash dummy of the Mafia. You didn't have to tell him but one time, and he was on it.

I wasn't too worried about anything. I was happy that I had accomplished what I wanted, and that was having Corey. I was even happier that Dollie hadn't answered her phone. The last thing I wanted was for him to be tied to her by way of her ride.

I had my sister pick my kids up from school for me, while I woke Tyrese and Karen up from their nap. When she arrived at my house with them, Corey still wasn't back. She came into the house and sat down in the living room with all the kids. I was in the kitchen, cooking some ribs.

"What you making?" she shouted from the living room.

"Ribs."

I began to take out the ingredients for the sides that I was going to make. I had to impress my new baby. Let him see what a real woman was capable of. Then, later on, I was going to give him some of this good pussy.

"Big sis is cooking it up, huh?" I could hear her say as she flipped through the channels on the TV.

I smiled to myself. After I was finished preparing the ribs and got them in the oven, I went into the living room. I began to tell Justine what had happened.

"So Bobbie's out, and Corey's in," she said when I was done. She paused briefly. "I don't have any problems with Corey. That's the homie."

"Oh yeah, sis? 'Cause on the cool Drew been kind of throwing shade," I confessed to my sister.

"Throwing shade how? Drew ain't no hater, sis. You know that." My sister laughed out loud.

"I don't mean a hater, sister. But he did give me a warning."

Justine shook her head in exasperation. We both knew how our brother was when it came to us. I mean, the three of us really went hard for one another, anyway. I just wished Drew's reaction to me wanting to be with Corey was one of pure excitement, like what he'd expressed when Bobbie and I first got together. My sister was making it clear to me, though, that she wasn't fixing to take sides, either. I told her about what he had said before they pinned me down on the ground.

"Look out, big sis," Justine said. "You know Drew is going to voice his opinion, no matter what. Just look at it as him trying to help you see clearly. Hell, I don't know. Emotions was running pretty high. Like you just up and decided Bobbie couldn't stay anymore. That was pretty wild, sis, and you know this."

All I could do was nod my head as if I understood. I decided to drop the conversation for now.

She and I both became engrossed in the old television series *The Golden Girls*. The aroma from the ribs baking in the oven had the whole house smelling good. I was going to make sure when everybody had a piece that they knew I had put my foot into this meal. As Justine and I watched *The Golden Girls*, our sides were throbbing with pain from laughing so hard. We had probably seen this show a thousand times, and we still giggled like it was the first time we had ever watched it.

During a commercial, I had checked on the ribs and put the potatoes on. Then I settled on the couch with my sister, and we debated whether or not to keep watching *The Golden Girls* or to catch the latest episode of *Music Moguls* on BET. Right then Corey, Bruce, and another young nigga from around the way came inside. My new boo stopped and gave me a kiss. Then he followed behind the other two as they entered the kitchen.

"They probably got some dope," Justine said.

"How do you know?" I knew I probably sounded naive.

She just shrugged her shoulders and focused her attention back on *Music Moguls*.

I knew what dope was, but I didn't have to be around it like Justine and Drew. My baby daddy had always taken care of me.

Even when he stopped loving me, he still chose to keep doing for me. He had made a choice to keep a roof over my head. I had never had to be subjected to that, not even when he was hustling. Now I was going to have to stand on my own. If that meant my feet had to get dirty in this game, so be it.

A few minutes later, Bruce and the young nigga emerged from the kitchen. He and the young nigga were both friends. Bruce motioned for my sister to come with them. She got up and left with them. Before she left, she made sure to let me know that I needed to save her some ribs.

Right after Justine left, Corey called me into the kitchen.

"These ribs smelling good, babe. How much longer?" He had the oven door open and was peeking at the ribs. I looked over at the clock and advised him that it was going to be another forty minutes before we could all eat. That was when the conversation turned a little serious.

"I know you used to a nigga taking care of you. I'm willing to do my part. But I need you to understand something. I gotta keep Dollie around. I doubt this will ever happen, 'cause I got to keep my game on point, but if it ever comes down to it and she asks you . . . I'm saying *if* she asks you about us, say we're just friends and I'm staying here because my pops and I are into it." His eyes were awfully humorless.

Mine were too, though. Like it pissed me off that I had to go along with this shit. Even though we did need a vehicle, I just wanted the bitch out of both of our lives. I wanted him, and I got him. Now we got to sit here and act like we ain't a couple so he could do what he needed to do to get the truck. I nodded my head to let him know I understood, when deep down inside I was simmering in fury.

Right after dinner was done and everybody had eaten, Corey helped me with getting the kids to bed. He handled the boys, and I took care of the girls. Then I washed the dishes and wiped the stove down. Right when I was finishing up, Corey wandered into the kitchen. I observed as Corey began to cook some dope. After he was done with the first half, he noticed I was still in the kitchen, watching his every step.

"What's up?" he asked as he lit a cigarette. "You don't mind, do you?" He had a concerned expression engraved on his face.

"Naw, baby. Just show me what you are doing," I demanded.

I quickly put up the ribs, and then I placed the potatoes and the green beans in containers. I put them in the fridge too. I cleared off the counter to make more space. When Corey realized I was dead-ass serious, he commenced to lace me up.

"All you need is a whisk, a measuring cup, baking soda, and a glass pot," he began.

He rummaged around until he discovered all that he was looking for, except for the glass pot. I didn't have a glass pot. He walked out of the kitchen and disappeared into my bedroom. He came back, holding a duffel bag. I stood in amazement as he pulled out a big glass pot.

I paid close attention as he revealed to me how to make some *drop*. By the time he was done, my head was spinning. A rush of eagerness came over me. Seeing him stretch the dope out so he could calculate exactly how much money he was going to make motivated me. I was also very interested in learning about a world that everybody in the vicinity appeared to be tangled in.

After we cleaned the mess created by cooking the powder up, I scrubbed down the areas of the kitchen we had used. While I was scrubbing, I overheard Corey on the phone. He was sitting at the kitchen table, rolling up a blunt.

"I'm back on, my nigga," I heard Corey say. "Let me hold something."

I finished making the kids' Kool-Aid for tomorrow, and then I made myself another plate. A couple of Corey's friends came through. They stood in the living room and talked in real low voices. When his homies left, I was sitting at the table, tearing through another piece of the ribs.

Corey walked into the kitchen. "Damn, baby. What about me?" he asked.

I got up and quickly made him a plate as well. We both sat down and ate. Corey schooled me on how to break the crack up into fragments. He then proceeded to tell me about the different quantities he packaged.

"If I'm out, I need you to be here so you can serve the ones who come to the door. Only our good clientele will know to come here," he instructed.

I listened, taking every word in. When we were through eating, I cleaned the kitchen up for the last time. Afterward, I checked on my kids to make sure they were all sound asleep.

Corey was on the phone, arguing, when I walked back into the living room. A bad feeling rushed through me. I shook it off, though. It sounded like he was talking to Dollie. A hint of jealousy crept through me. But I reminded myself that all he wanted from her was her truck. He could ride in it all he wanted, as long as he was about me and my kids. If she wanted to be a dummy behind him, then so be it. We would both play her weak ass like a fiddle.

I was down for the ride. *Fuck that girl.*

Chapter 16

Dollie

Our stay at Corey's mom's house ended rather abruptly. We had made plans to have brunch with Tiger's family after church, but thanks to my so-called *infidelity*, we had cut that shit short. Instead we left Corey's mom's house first thing Sunday morning. I had to make him get his ass up, because I was ready to go home. I refused to stay at the house of anybody who assumed the first piece of bullshit they heard was the absolute truth. I did not appreciate one bit being accused of some fucked-up shit that I didn't do. Naomi clearly was the type of chick who was miserable and liked it when everybody else was too. For her to downright lie like that pissed me off. I hadn't been able to sleep a wink last night because of this. I wanted to go home.

The story was that I had cheated on Corey with one of his homeboys. Apparently, Michael, their dad, had told Naomi because he didn't want to be the one to let Corey know, but even this fact turned out to be false. When I heard that, I immediately called Michael and asked him about it. I was so irate that I put him on speakerphone and let him in on the bullshit that was being said about me. Michael was so infuriated about this lie that he ended up cussing out Brenda and Corey.

That night, Corey said, I started a bunch of unnecessary shit, when really it was his sister. Something deep down inside told me that this was going to be the ultimate reason and excuse for him to do whatever he damn well pleased. His corny-ass sister was fucking with my relationship, and I was not too happy about that at all.

The fact that he believed what she had said and did not speak with me before drawing conclusions hurt me to the core. So, in my mind, I was through with him. I was done with his sister and his mom too. His grandma had warned me about how crazy his white side of the family was. I was the type who liked to judge things for myself. Now I knew I should have listened to his grandma.

We drove the two hours back to Abilene in silence. Drake was sleeping in his car seat. Corey was pretending to be asleep. I knew better, and I was well aware that he liked to start drama but didn't like to finish it. I was pretty pissed off and disappointed that he didn't seem bothered at all that our relationship was on the rocks. We had been doing so fucking well, and then shit had hit the fan based on some bullshit, and now it was like "Fuck you."

I was feeling like I had really exhausted my energy waiting on him. At the same time a giant part of me just aspired to make shit right again, to take him by the shoulders and shake his ass super hard, make him want to listen to me, make him see that it was a bunch of lies. We were stronger than this. We could pull through this. Unfortunately, it was not enough that I just want it. He had to want to make shit work too.

I dropped him off at his grandma's house and peeled out of the driveway when I was sure he had got all his bags. His dad came outside, talking shit, I was sure. I kept right on going. I was drained by the circumstances and just needed to get as far away as I could.

When I reached my aunt and uncle's house, I detected that neither one of them was there. However, my cousin Victoria was there. Her dark purple Volkswagen Beetle was parked in the driveway, in the spot where my uncle normally parked his car. I pulled up in front of the house and brought my son inside first.

Drake saw Victoria talking on the cordless phone in the den and made a beeline toward her as soon as I put him down. When I saw that she had spotted him, I went outside and carried in our things. When I was finished, I had made my son a bowl of Malt-o-Meal and fixed myself a cup of coffee.

I sat at the kitchen table and tried to squelch the feelings of hatred I felt toward Corey's mom and his crazy sister. That girl had no right lying her ass off like that. His mom was ignorant for believing that shit. That was one family who reacted first and asked questions later. I was truly dumbfounded at this moment.

I stared off into space, deep in thought. I was reviewing the ongoing confrontation in my mind and trying to make sense of everything at the same damn time. I was so lost in thought that I didn't notice when my big cousin took a seat next to me. Finally, I looked up and was struck by her thick, curly hair, which was dyed blond and had light red streaks in it. On anybody else, that hair might have looked crazy, but my cousin, she was beautiful with that combination.

"Earth to Doll. Earth to Doll. Can you hear me now?" my cousin teased, waving her hands vigorously in front of my face. She had a huge grin displayed on her adorable face. I snapped back to reality and flashed a smile at her.

"What are you doing here, Vic?" I asked her as I took a sip of my coffee.

"I have about five loads of laundry to do." She rolled her eyes. "Dad gave me the day off. At first, I was pretty pissed off about it. I needed it, anyway. I stayed in the back all day yesterday, baking all them damn birthday cakes for him."

As she went on about the day she had had at work yesterday, I removed Drake's empty bowl from the kitchen table, then cut him up a banana to eat. He loved eating fruit after his breakfast. I also filled his sippy cup with grape juice.

My cousin could cook. Despite the fact that she had never been able to keep a man due to her drug addiction, her place was in the kitchen. That was one thing nobody could take away from my cousin. She had always wanted to be a chef. That was her main dream. Another thing my cousin could do was bake. Vic treasured her time baking too.

She looked at me as I sat down. "How'd your trip go?"

I took a sip of my coffee and stared at her. I debated for a minute whether or not to tell her what had happened. She was rather close to my aunt, and I knew she would go back and tell her. I really wanted to talk about it, though. I had been blowing up my best friend, but she wasn't answering her cell phone at all. Theoretically, I could wait for her to call back, but this shit was driving me insane. I had to get it out. So I took a deep breath and told her every detail.

As I was talking, I took Drake out of his big boy seat. Without my asking her, Victoria got up and cleared the table at the same time that she listened to me gab. As soon as I was through, she shook her head in disappointment. I couldn't blame her. I was feeling quite defeated right about now.

"I'm so outraged right now. Seriously frustrated that he would listen to her over me. I did more for him than they ever did the whole time he was locked up!" I screeched, unable to contain my resentment.

"Girl, fuck that shit. You are better than me. I would have given that Brenda something to be mad about. And his damn sister. Who is the person you supposedly slept with?"

"That's what I kept asking, and *nobody* could tell me who this individual is," I stated.

"Exactly. I would have read the shit out they asses." You could tell when Victoria got mad. Her Spanish accent really stood out.

"I can't be with him like that. I won't move to Bedford now. You should have seen how chaotic it was when we got there. If that's what it was like the day I stayed there, I can only picture what kind of bullshit occurs day in and day out."

"Doll, you don't need that," she said softly, sympathizing with my plight. "You go to law school, girl. Ignore Corey. He's going to go back to jail sooner or later. His ass ain't changed. He still runs with that gang, and he's back to selling dope again."

I felt myself cringe when she told me that. Needing a time-out to gather my thoughts, I walked out of the kitchen to go check on my son, who had wandered into the hallway. He was sitting on the floor, content with playing with Victoria's empty laundry basket. I walked back into the kitchen to find Victoria rummaging around in the freezer. I was dying to know how she knew Corey was selling drugs again. And I really wanted to know if she was using again.

"You know that for sure?" I asked.

Victoria stopped what she was doing and looked at me. I already knew that Corey had seized the opportunity to sell dope on a few occasions since his release from prison. It allowed him to make a little bit of money here and there. But I thought he had stopped pushing that shit full-time, the way he used to. Stopped being real deep into the streets and shit. His getting back into that fast life was not something that was a part of our plans. However, sometimes our plans didn't unfold the way we wanted them to. I was starting to experience that firsthand.

"I ain't lying, girl. That's the word on the street. He just hasn't started selling it the way he used to yet. But it's coming. These niggas just don't get their feet wet a little bit. That money draws them in. It's an addiction to them. Just like how that cocaine draws me in, the money does the same thing. Gives them a high," she explained.

I felt my heart break right then. This whole time he had been lying to me. His so-called looking for jobs and shit was him looking for his old clientele. Him finding them drug dealers and bangers to constantly re-up with. That lifestyle was something I definitely didn't want to be a part of any longer.

"Don't get your panties in a wad. Cheer up, cousin," Victoria told me. "Let him show you what kind of man he turned out to be. He'll either surprise you or disappoint you. Like Maya Angelou says, when a person shows you who they are, believe them."

She was right. Her words made me feel a bit better. At the same time they also made my anxiety act up a little more. The waiting game. It seemed like all I ever did with this man was wait. Wait for the good Corey to reappear. Wait for Corey to get out of jail. Now I had to wait to see if he was going to do the right thing or become a victim once again to these streets? I was tired of waiting on a man to figure out that he wanted to start being a man.

My aunt Audrina called just then to let us know she was going to be at the bakery for a little bit longer, doing payroll and helping my uncle out. Victoria decided to make them some homemade lasagna while she did her laundry. She was also going to bake an angel cake, and for Drake, she would whip up some homemade chocolate chip cookies.

Victoria agreed to keep an eye on my son while I lay down for a little bit. I was beginning to get a headache from all that thinking I was doing. I was debating with myself about this relationship. I was torn between saying, "Fuck it," and working things out. I just didn't see why I had to work anything out when it was his sister who had lied like that. He should be the one kissing my ass, not the other way around.

I was woken up an hour later, when my best friend, Jazzy, finally called. She was Filipino and white. We both had attended high school together. She'd moved out of town to go to Baylor, where she was currently studying to be a doctor. She was short like me and very petite. She had curly black hair that went past her shoulders. Some of my friends and acquaintances had fallen off when we graduated from high school, but Jazzy had continuously kept in contact.

When I answered the phone, Jazzy's cheerful voice flooded through the line, piercing my brain. She just made my head hurt even worse. I grabbed my Excedrin and yelled for Victoria to bring me some juice.

"Damn. You don't sound happy to hear from me," Jazzy said, then laughed at me.

I mumbled that she should give me one minute, and I instructed her not to hang up. A few second later, Victoria brought me some grape juice. I sat up, and I quickly swallowed two pills with it. Then I placed the juice on my nightstand and lay back down. I grabbed the phone and covered my whole head with the covers.

"I was resting, girl. Horrible weekend," I muttered.

"Your beautiful weekend wasn't paradise for the young wifey and her 'fresh out of lock' husband?" she teased me.

I cringed at her playful sarcasm. "Fresh out of lock" husband, huh? To shut her up, I told her about the whole weekend. I loved my Jazzy. She was always attentive. She was consistently open-minded, and she never talked down. She was like me. She came to me for advice as well, and I treated her the very same way she treated me.

"I love Corey. I really do," I told her. "I wouldn't have stood by his side if I didn't. But I fuckin' hate his family. Tiger ain't like that at all. I like Tiger, but Naomi was way out of line." I found myself sounding defensive.

I could feel my body become wide awake and alert. I listened intently for any sounds in the house, and I heard Victoria and Drake singing songs that played on the Disney Channel. I knew he was alive, well, and breathing.

"Now, things ain't always glorified with your in-laws," my best friend warned. "Maybe somebody told Naomi that."

"Like who? Nobody fucks with that girl like that. She hasn't lived her in years," I said.

"That doesn't mean anything, Dollie. People are sneaky and vindictive."

I quickly shut that down. I just didn't want any further discussion of Naomi. I just couldn't see why somebody would sit there and go out of their way to call somebody who wasn't that important to them. I mean, she did know people, but nobody thought of Naomi like that. And it didn't make sense that Naomi would be watching out for Corey in this way. He loved his sister, but he rode for the streets harder than he did for some of his own family members. When I told Jazzy, she took a deep breath.

"I can see why you are mad. But maybe he was just hurt by it all."

"That man wasn't hurt. He went with the flow. I feel like a random bum could walk up to him and feed him some bullshit and he'd eat that shit up." I could feel myself getting angry again.

"A random bum?"

"Yes, girl. He's going to use that as an excuse to start acting up again. Watch." I was firm about that.

My friend took a deep breath before she began talking again. "Just give it a couple of days. See what happens then. My advice to you, Dollie, is that if you guys don't have trust, you really don't have a ground to stand on in your relationship."

I had to admit, Jazzy was right. There was no room to build a solid foundation if the ground was made of lies. If the other one wasn't fully in it like you were. I needed to figure out which road I needed to take. At this point, considering how deeply involved I was right about now, it was either going to hurt to stay or hurt to leave. The choice was mine.

Chapter 17

It had been a couple of days since I spoke to Corey. He had called me, but I had just refused to answer his calls. On Wednesday afternoon, Jerry gave me the rest of the day off. It had been a rather slow day, and I had finished everything that needed to be done. The day had been so leisurely that I had resorted to cleaning the bathroom from top to bottom and rearranging the kitchen area.

Furthermore, Tammy was in the office, and she could answer the phones while she finished his closing arguments for his court date on Friday. Jerry planned to be in the office, too, as he had meetings there all afternoon, until about four, and then he was going to go to the jailhouse in Anson to talk to a potential client. It was one of those rare days in weeks when he had to spend only half a day in court. And another good thing was that his morning in court had been spent right across the street from us, in the courthouse here in Abilene.

Without hesitation, I grabbed my Manolo shades and walked out the front door. I decided to go to the salon to get a back rub, a manicure, and a pedicure. I called my cousin to see what she was doing. She was just getting home from the bakery, and she agreed to meet me at Vendettas Salon and Day Spa.

She pulled up behind me at the salon within minutes of my arrival there. We used to do things like this all the time a few years back. That was before I had figured out she was a drug addict. I knew she didn't smoke it at all anymore. And if she did, then it wasn't hardly as much as she used to. I guessed I wouldn't put it past her if she did smoke every once in a while.

My cousin walked in the salon, looking incredible. She had her blue jean capris on with a Chanel tube top shirt. She had straightened her hair, and her long blond and red-streaked locks gleamed radiantly against her smooth light skin. We waited for five minutes, chatting like two teenage girls, before they called us back.

We relaxed in the salon and were pampered for a good hour and a half. When we were done, Victoria had to go run some errands. I decided to go to Whataburger to get something to eat before I picked my little boy up. I wanted to enjoy the feeling after that good rubdown I had just had.

When I pulled up to the Whataburger on First Street, I saw that the drive-through line was too long. I parked my truck in the parking lot and headed inside to place my order. I was the third person in line when I walked in. Right when I was placing my order, I noticed out of the corner of my eye that Drew, Bruce, and Bruce's wife were walking in. I instantly froze up. Then I shook it off. I opted to pretend as if I didn't see them.

I paid for my order and walked over to the soda fountain and filled my cup up with orange soda. When I turned around, Bruce was ordering his food. His wife was standing beside him like an obedient guard dog. Drew was heading toward me. Before I could say hi, he gave me a big ole hug. It was unexpected and a nice gesture. I had to admit I was cheesing at this point.

"How are you doing, Doll?" His handsome smile hypnotized me for a brief second, but I shook that off and smiled back.

"Just great. Just enjoying my afternoon off."

We stood around and chatted for a bit. They called my number, and I grabbed my to-go bag and drink and said my good-byes. It wasn't until I had got in my truck and had pulled out of the parking lot that it dawned on me how odd Bruce and his girl had been acting. Normally, Bruce would say hi, but he hadn't this time. Usually, his girl would speak too, but Justine hadn't said anything. She'd looked a little nervous. How weird was that?

I pulled up to my house and grabbed my food and drink. I walked around to the backyard so I could eat my food on the patio. I decided to not dwell on Bruce's and Justine's odd behavior, even though it was kind of messed up that they hadn't acknowledged me. It kind of pissed me off. I had always spoken to that man when I saw him. I made a mental note to bring up his behavior the next time I saw him. I had thought we were better than that, but it was all good.

As I finished my hamburger, an unknown number called my cell. I declined the call. I leaned back in the lawn chair I was sitting in. It was very nice outside. There weren't any flies buzzing around. The temperature was perfect. Not too hot or too cold. Just nice. Right then my phone rang again. The same number popped up. I forwarded the call to my voice mail once again. Immediately after that, the phone rang again. This time I answered; then I took a drink of my soda.

"What's up, baby?" Corey was on the other end.

What the fuck? I was still mad at him. Very, very mad. But the sound of his voice filled my heart with this amazingly crazy feeling. A huge part of me was ready to reconcile, work through the mess, and put it behind us. I wanted to move forward with him.

"Where you at?" I demanded. I had to focus on being upset so I wouldn't let my joy show through.

"Damn. No 'I love you'? No callin' me baby today?"

"I said, 'Where you are?'" I questioned.

"I'm over here, at my aunt Torie's. My cell phone died. I need a new charger." When I didn't reply, he continued on. "We need to talk."

"You damn right we do. I just ain't sure what I want to do, so I just need more time to speak." Before Corey could reply, I kept going. "I came to visit you in jail, and I put money on your books. We were becoming so close. Then your sister says one thing, and you start trippin'. One fucking thing. Maybe our bond wasn't as tight as I thought it was. Or maybe deep down inside, you didn't want this like I did. That's why your ass believed her so easily."

"Say, she ain't the only one who said that," Corey said, defending his sister.

"Who said it, then, Corey? Where is all this bullshit coming from? Who is the person?"

"You know who the person is!" he yelled.

Was he trying me right now? My stomach was turning. I was beginning to fill up with anger again. How dare this piece of shit call me and still not be able to come up with a name?

"Who is it?" I demanded again.

"The streets is talking, Dollie. Stop trying to play innocent."

"Oh, so now the streets are talking, but there ain't no fuckin' name of the person I was supposedly fuckin' with? They couldn't say hello when you were in jail? But they want to deliver some fuckin' news about me now? Real nice, Corey. Fuck you and the streets." I hung up on him.

Suddenly, I wasn't in the mood to eat the rest of my fries. I sat there for a minute, going over the argument in my head. I took a glimpse at the time on my phone. It was getting close to the time I had to go get my son. I carried my food to the Dumpster, chucked it, and then took off to the day care.

When I got there, instead of going to get my son, I headed straight to my aunt's office. My aunt Audrina was having a conversation over the phone that sounded somewhat important. But when she saw the look on my face, she advised the person she was speaking to that she'd call him or her back. She hung up the phone, with no questions asked.

"Oh, mija. Que está pasando?"

I wasn't no genius in Spanish, but I knew enough little shit to understand the simple things my aunt would say. She had said this same thing throughout my younger years. I knew exactly what she was saying. I stole one look at my aunt's alarmed face and burst into tears.

She motioned for me to take a seat, and then she quietly got up and left her office, closing the door behind her. I didn't mind being left alone at all. I needed to get these tears out, though. She returned fifteen minutes later. She gave me a big hug and rubbed the back of my neck.

"I told Ms. Kayla that you were here. I made Drake a bowl of banana pudding, so he can eat while we talk."

I reached over for a Kleenex and wiped my nose. I told her what had happened, starting with the weekend at Corey's mom's down to our last conversation. I was pretty sure she already knew about it. Victoria couldn't hold hot water at all. She had to tell somebody. I had known better before even saying anything to Victoria, but I'd had to get it out. I'd had to let somebody know my suffering.

"If he feels that negatively, Doll, let him go," my aunt said. Her voice was stern yet loving. "You are too beautiful to go through this. I don't understand why you young girls put yourselves through all this nonsense. Life is too short for this."

"I don't get it, Aunt Audrina. Why is he acting like that? If he doesn't want me, why can't he be a man, instead of playing with my head? I feel so stupid for wasting my time on that boy."

My aunt shook her head at me. "You're not stupid. God put you through this for a reason. If anybody is making a mistake, baby girl, it's him. God don't like ugly. Trust me on that. Whatever he puts out there has to come back to him sooner or later."

Her words were comforting. She was all I had to go to for wisdom, since my mother was no longer around. I appreciated my aunt for taking the time out to listen to me. Especially when she had a business to run and other things to tend to. We talked for a few more minutes, and then I kissed my aunt good-bye.

Before I left, I went to pick up my son. Luckily for me, he had finished his pudding. We left, and I took him straight to my aunt and uncle's house. I didn't take him by the bakery, because he still had a few cookies left from the batch that Victoria had made.

My uncle Justin was already there and was in the backyard, firing up the pit. I quickly went and cleaned up my face. I put some Visine in my eyes to hide the redness. I hated having talks with my uncle. He lectured me too much. I knew my aunt would tell him what was going on with me, but he'd say what he had to say to her, and that would be that.

I played with my son for an hour and a half in the den. When my aunt arrived, Drake headed over to her. Drake and my aunt were really close. He was also close to his grandma, his dad's mom.

Drake's dad had passed away after a bad car accident when I was seven months pregnant. So, all that Drake's paternal grandma had left of her own son was her grandson, my son. He was the closest thing to her son she and I had left. I would never deprive her of the chance to spend time with her grandson. She generally picked him up on the holidays and every other weekend, if her job allowed. She worked for an advertising firm, so whenever she had a day off, Drake was with her.

My aunt scooped up Drake and walked into the backyard to greet my uncle. Right then, my phone rang again. Before checking to see who was calling, I answered it absentmindedly. It was Corey again.

"I don't want to talk right now, Corey—" I began to say, but he interrupted me.

"But listen to me, Dollie—"

I hung up the phone. For thirty minutes straight he called me nonstop. Every time I forwarded his call, he'd start right back up. I gave in. I completely caved in.

"Damn! What do you want?" I yelled into the phone.

"Say, man, just come outside."

I hung up the cell phone and ran to the front door, hoping my aunt and uncle wouldn't see me. I was furious that he would just come over without asking me if it was okay. When I got outside, Corey was standing by the truck. A wave of confusion came over me. I walked around to the edge of the yard and looked down the street.

"How'd you get here?" I turned around as I walked in his direction.

He shrugged his shoulders and looked at me. "One of the homies dropped me off. What's up, man?"

I looked down at the grass and shook my head. This was unbelievable. I didn't know what to make of all of this. I knew I wanted these ill feelings I was having to leave me. If that meant saying good-bye to him, then so be it. But having this man stand before me pulled on my heartstrings. I really, *really* wanted to make shit work. The real question was, did he?

"Let's just put all this shit behind us. I really need to use the truck, though. Some shit went down between me and my pops. I'm having to stay with Drew's sister, Tenosha, until I can find some place to go. You need to get a house, baby. Real talk," Corey aid.

I glared at him, stared blankly. I didn't understand why he would have to leave his grandma's house. He and his dad had had an argument? Okay. Cool. Corey was hardly there, anyway, during the day. He could easily avoid his dad by only sleeping there at night, like he'd been doing. I didn't see how they could have been arguing so bad that he just had to leave. Why did this story not sit well with me?

"You left your grandma's?" I was really smelling *bullshit* written all over this.

"You know me and my pops don't get along. He was tripping, so I had to drop his ass. He called my PO on me and everything."

"But for what? What were you arguing about, though?"

For every question I asked, he gave me an answer. I wasn't 100 percent satisfied with what he was dishing out. I had to learn to trust him again. I pulled my keys out of my pocket and asked him when he would bring the truck back. He told me that it would not be until much later, but he'd call my cell. He gave me a quick kiss and took off in my truck.

Chapter 18

Corey had been using my truck more often. He'd used it while I was at work, and sometimes, he'd kept it overnight. I had started to realize that our relationship was changing. Our conversations were short and simple now. And we had completely stopped having sex. I was beginning to think that he was cheating on me, but I couldn't figure out with whom.

A couple of days ago, Corey and I had ended up having an argument about him not filling the truck up with gas after he used it. It had ended with me telling him that I would not let him use the truck any longer. I hadn't called Corey since the argument. Even though I was mad at him, he was still on my mind a lot. Although he had been treating me badly, I was still in love with him. I wasn't ready to say good-bye to him, let alone move on to another man, but I knew I had to do it. I just needed to break through that feeling of attachment and let him go. I had to admit that a part of me really didn't want anybody else to have him.

It was a Wednesday, and my son was with his grandma for the week. She had taken him to a family reunion in Alabama. At work, Tammy invited me to go to a place called the Pub, which was a bar and grill. Wednesday night was ladies' night, and they had great drink specials for women, so I agreed to go. Tammy was going to pick me up at my place at eight.

Since Tammy and I were going out tonight, Jerry agreed to let us come in at noon tomorrow. He was going to be at the office in the morning, and he was sure he could manage the phone without us. Since I knew I didn't have to come in until noon tomorrow, I pushed myself extra hard to get tomorrow morning's work done. That left me with the peace of mind that came from knowing I wouldn't have too much to catch up on. Plus, my boss wouldn't have to do too much of my job for me.

After work, I went home to get ready to go out. I curled my hair and let the curls fall gracefully down my back. I lightly applied some makeup on my face, and a dash of J.Lo's Glow perfume behind my ears and knees and on my wrists. I put on a white halter dress that showed off my curvy, small body. I slipped into some red heels and attached red hoop earrings to my ears. Then I put a red clip in my hair. By eight o' clock, I was ready to go, and Tammy was outside in her Beamer, waiting on me.

I hurried down the hall. I passed by the kitchen and heard a long whistle. It was my aunt giving me her signature stamp of approval. I posed, as if I was having my picture taken. Then I kissed my aunt good-bye and headed out the door.

"Girl, you look sexy!" Tammy growled at me from her car as I approached.

"You don't look too bad yourself, beautiful!" I complimented her back as I slid into the passenger seat.

Tammy did look wonderful, as always. She had on a black, short-sleeved cashmere shirt and a pair of white skinny jeans. She wore black heels, and a string of white beads hung around her neck. She also had on some green contacts, which stood out against her fiery red hair.

We pulled up at the Pub within minutes. The parking lot was halfway full. We parked, went inside, and immediately headed toward the bar. We both got a glass of

Hennessy and Coke. I also took a bottle of Corona, and Tammy got a bottle of Miller Light.

We headed to a table toward the back, where the grill was. Within minutes, our table was surrounded by potential bachelors, guys who had girlfriends, and playboys. I had to admit, Tammy and I were having so much fun that the liquor soon made me forget all about my boy problems.

One of the guys brought us some nachos to eat. They all took their turns grilling us for information on our private lives. We both took delight in giving them the wrong information about us. I thought they knew it too, because we were equally dying from laughter.

I decided to go dance with one of the guys, the one who had bought me a Slippery Nipple shot. I was dipping down and shaking it low while Waka Flocka's song "No Hands" blared from the speakers. When I came back up, I saw Corey walk through the door with his arm around a pudgy light-skinned girl. From a distance, she looked like a dirty Mexican. She had pulled her hair back in a high ponytail, and all she wore was a white tee and black jeans. I felt my heart drop, and although I knew I was drunk, I felt myself sober up real fast.

I immediately stopped dancing and stomped over to where Tammy was sitting. She was engaged in a conversation with an Asian guy who looked like he was in the military. He smiled at me, but I was too drunk and heated to acknowledge him back. I tapped Tammy's shoulder, and when she looked up, I pointed at the front door. Together, we watched Corey and his lady friend walk over to a table. Right behind them were Bruce and his wife. *Double date, huh?* This nigga thought he was slick. This was what had been going on behind my back. I looked over at Tammy, and she looked at me.

"He's got some nerve, Doll. Who the hell is she?"

"I bet you it's whoever he's been acting funny with me about."

"Are you two over?" She looked at me closely.

"We are now," I said to her.

"Does *he* know that?" She pointed her finger in their direction.

We both watched. I felt a level of boldness spread within me. This was the straw that had just broken the camel's back. I knew that sensible Dollie had left the building. I was about to show my ass. He was fixing to learn today that fuckin' with me and my emotions was a huge no-no.

"I don't know, but I think we ought to make that clear," I replied.

I turned to the table and quickly chugged down the Budweiser one of the guys had sent over to me. I needed the extra juice to calm my nerves. I removed my heels and immediately began to tramp across the dance floor, pulling my hair back in a ponytail as I went. Tammy followed right behind me. Even the guys who had been standing around us and had caught wind of our conversation were following close behind, with their nosy asses.

When I approached Corey's table, I saw Bruce kick Corey under the table. Corey and his girlfriend had been looking at something on his cell phone. Bruce and his girl, Justine, stood up, like they was getting ready to do something. Justine eyed Tammy, but the firmness in Tammy's stance showed me she wasn't backing down to anybody. I was so damn glad she was with me and had my back 100 percent.

I grabbed the glass that sat in front of Bruce. He tried unsuccessfully to intercede, but I stepped out of his reach. When Corey turned to face me, I threw the contents of the glass all over him.

"This is the whore you been cheating on me with?" I shouted at him. "That fat, lumpy, Oompa-Loompa-lookin'-ass bitch!"

I hurtled insult after insult, destroying this bitch's self-esteem. Or doing my best to, anyway. I was disgusted by his latest choice. She had better be half the woman I was, because by the looks of it, he had traded in his Benz for a beat-up Buick.

"Man, bitch! What the fuck?" Corey stood up.

Before he had a chance to grab me, I grabbed their table and flipped that ho over. *Bitch?* I was about to show him exactly what this bitch was about.

"Fuck you!" I yelled at him.

I had seen the pudgy girl act like she was going to rush me, so I turned to face her. "What, bitch?" I threw my hands up at her, and she quickly backed up.

Tammy let me know that security was making its way over. I threw one more dirty look at Corey, shot him the middle finger, yelled from the top of my lungs that I was done with his dusty ass, and followed Tammy out of the club.

Chapter 19

By the next morning news had traveled around Abilene about my run-in with Corey. He had called my phone one thousand times, but I had my ringer off. I woke up around ten and hopped in the shower. Then I brewed myself a cup of coffee while I finished getting ready for work. As I sat down in the living room to drink my coffee and read the paper, my cousin Victoria came into my aunt and uncle's house.

Victoria headed in the direction of my bedroom, bypassing me altogether. When she came back into the living room, I knocked twice on the coffee table. She was so dingy, I had to laugh. How had she not seen me sitting right here? The laughing was short lived, though. The throbbing in my head only got worse when I chuckled.

When she spotted me, she blurted out, "What the hell happened?"

I shushed her, signaling to her that I had a slight hangover. She instantly walked over to where I was sitting and plopped down right beside me.

She lowered her voice. "It's all over Abilene. You showed the fuck out at the Pub. How'd you find out?"

I took a sip of the bitter black coffee and pursed my lips. A bit of confusion coursed through me. I needed clarification on that question she had just asked me. I hoped my own fuckin' family member wasn't asking me what I thought she was.

"What you mean?" I said.

Vic's eyes grew big. She knew she had just made a big mistake. My eyes were trained on her. She was going to let me know today what the hell she meant by what she had just said. How could something be all over Abilene that I had supposedly found out about when I didn't even fucking know what the hell she was talking about? What the hell had she meant when she said that?

"How'd you find out Corey was fuckin' with Ten?" she said.

"What the hell you mean, Vic? Who the fuck is Ten?"

I was beginning to get very upset again. But as my mood worsened, the pounding in my head did as well. I had a funny feeling in the pit of my stomach about who this Ten chick was. I had a funny feeling that this Ten bitch was that Tenosha bitch he had claimed he was staying with due to his daddy putting him out. How the fuck could I be so blind to his bullshit!

"Tenosha, that chick Corey moved in with. I thought it was a rumor, because you hadn't mentioned it. Then I saw Corey, Bruce, Majesta, and Tenosha in your truck one night, selling dope out of it," Victoria revealed.

Bingo! I narrowed my eyes at her. This so-called *man* I was with had been playing me for an ain't-nothing-ass dope girl? My own family had known about it and hadn't even told me? Victoria had seen that nigga selling drugs out of my fuckin' transportation and hadn't even called and given me a heads-up? What type of shit was that? I didn't know if I should be upset that he was dogging me the fuck out for trash in the yard or if I should be angry that she hadn't even told me this when this shit first popped off and she saw it live, in the flesh.

"Victoria! How the fuck you know all this shit and ain't said one word?" I screamed at her. That made my headache worse.

I got up and immediately called Tammy. I asked her if she could handle my workload for me if I called in. When she gave me the assurance that she could, I called Jerry to let him know I wasn't going to be in. I hardly ever called in to work. When I had to, though, Jerry never asked questions. He was family oriented, which was a major plus for me. The fact that he was like this was something I never took advantage of. However, today skipping work was a must. I wasn't going to be able to be productive with all this extra shit going on around me.

"Man, I'm sorry, Dollie. I didn't think you wanted to know that."

"Fuck that, Vic. He disrespected me. As a matter of fact, that ho-ass nigga been doing this shit and clowning me behind my back while everybody smiles in my face like nothing is even going on. So now I need to even the score. Last night wasn't enough."

"I'm coming with you. I don't have to go to the bakery until four."

I went into my bedroom and quickly grabbed two Excedrins. I headed to the kitchen, took the Excedrins with some water, and poured some coffee into a Styrofoam cup so I could continue to nurse my hangover. Headache or not, everybody was about to feel my pain.

"Let's ride to the neighborhood. I'm jumping out on the first ho out of that group I see," I told my cousin.

Victoria and I got into her Beetle and headed over to the hood that One Tre Mafia ran. We rode up and down the streets for about thirty minutes and kept passing by Tenosha's house. It looked like either nobody was there or they weren't coming outside anytime soon. Two blocks down, my cousin pulled her car over and pointed at a real bright-skinned female. She was standing outside, talking on a cordless phone.

"Remember her? She's Majesta, one of Ten's real good friends," Victoria informed me.

That was all my cousin had to say. I exited the car and instantaneously ran up on her. Majesta saw me and slowly backed up in the direction of her front door.

"Don't say shit to me," I yelled. I could feel my voice get higher and higher. "You fuck with Tenosha? That bitch has been in my ride, and from what I hear, you were too. What's up? You bitches can't afford to get your own shit? You think that shit is cute to sell work out my shit? A vehicle I grind my ass off to keep and maintain?"

"It ain't even like that—" Majesta began, but I cut her off.

"Don't explain yourself. I ain't mad at you. You let your little homegirl know that if she was any kind of a woman, she'd come holla at me. As a matter of fact, if Corey was any kind of a man, he should have kept it real from the gate. Your little nothing-ass friend will have to see me one day. Bet on that." I turned around and got back into my cousin's ride.

We drove off and stopped at the gas station on the Mafia's territory. My cousin jumped out and went inside to pay for her gas. I stayed behind, trying to calm my nerves down. Just then, I saw Drew and his girlfriend pull up at the tank beside mine. He got out, ready to pump. Koa walked inside to pay. I got out of the car and walked over to him. Tenosha was Drew's sister, which meant he knew what was going on. I could feel myself getting irate by the minute as I put all the pieces to this infidelity together. The number of individuals who knew or were involved was embarrassingly fucked up.

Drew saw me coming, and he started to speak. The look on my face silenced him. He didn't ignore me after that, and no matter if he wanted to talk about things or not, I had questions to ask. I deserved answers. I broke the ice, beating him to the punch and speaking first.

"I guess we weren't ever friends," I stated, watching him closely.

"Dollie, it wasn't my place to tell you."

I laughed hysterically at him in a fake, sarcastic way. "I'm sure. Out of all his friends, I liked you the most. I thought you were a friend of mine. Now I see you tiptoeing around, trying to hide relationships from me. So we ain't friends?" I stood there, waiting for him to reply, but he just shook his head.

"That's my sister, and that's my homeboy. I'm cool with you too, but damn. That wasn't my business to interfere like that. I got my own damn problems." The pump turned on for Drew, and he began to put gas in his car.

My cousin came out of the store, and following closely behind her was Drew's girl. I knew Koa was real catty. I didn't give a damn, though. Today was not the day for her psycho ass to be fucking with me. Given the way I was feeling, anybody who popped off could get it.

"Don't we all got problems? Sucks for you," I sneered at him.

As I turned to head back to my ride, Drew called my name.

I looked back at him. "What, Mr. Problems of My Own?"

"For what it's worth, Doll, I'm sorry you had to go through all that. If you were my girl, I wouldn't treat you like that. I really am sorry."

"Aren't we all?" I responded as I slid into the passenger-side seat.

I was shocked about what Drew had said, and I instantly thought about apologizing to him. Taking it all back. Just like that, though, I abandoned that thought. I did have to be a rational thinker. Nobody could make a grown-ass person do something they didn't want to do, whether it was right, wrong, or indifferent. Just like I had

family, that girl was his sister. At the end of the day, my
anger was not meant for him. But I figured I would run
into him again when tensions were not so high. I would
take back the retort I had flung at him then.

When Vic was done pumping the gas, she got back in
the car and took me back to the house. After she dropped
me off, I let myself back into the house and locked myself
in the refuge of my bedroom. I called my son to speak
with him for a minute. It was good to know that at least
somebody loved me. After I hung up with his grandma, I
turned my cell phone off. I took off my clothes and put on
a night T-shirt. I cut on my TV and got under my covers.

That was when the humiliation really hit me. Mor-
tification over being played flooded through me. The
burning truth tore through my heart, as if somebody
was deliberately stabbing me over and over again with a
butcher knife. The pain I felt was unbearable, but it hurt
like hell only on the inside.

The emotional pain I felt from the wound forming in
my heart shot through me, and I tried so hard to fight
back the tears. My mind was telling me that Corey wasn't
worth it. My heart was truly damaged, because I loved
him. His betrayal had destroyed me. His impudence and
dishonesty had slaughtered me inside. I couldn't do it
anymore. I turned the volume up on my TV and buried
my face in my pillow. There I sobbed until I fell into a
bottomless sleep. Anything to escape the throbbing of my
injured heart.

Chapter 20

Tenosha

Corey, Majesta, and I were eating at the Taco Bell restaurant in Eastland. Bobbie had the kids for the week, so I didn't have to hurry back home. Corey had met a new connect through one of his big homies. The guy he was going to go through would travel only as far as Eastland. That meant when it was time to re-up, we were going to have to hop on that highway and drive here. His product was good, and it was guaranteed to bring in the money, so we were down for whatever.

I was starting to get the hang of this dope game. Some of Corey's licks called my phone. I would often make the deliveries by myself whenever shit got too busy and hectic. Most of the time when our clientele was not blowing us up, I'd be with Corey. When we didn't have a babysitter for the kids, I'd stay home, and Corey would go with Majesta or my brother-in-law. On those occasions I had to handle our good clientele, those who were allowed to come to the house. We were selling four bars and tabs, and I would handle the pills from the house. The homies were always on them. They were always looking for some, and since we now always had them, they pretty much became our customers. It was easy money and a no-brainer.

Corey seemed to be happy with me. He was always buying me things. I always had a new pair of Jordans or the latest Nikes. I was able to get my toes and fingernails done whenever I wanted. And the best part was, I did not have to work. I also saw a big difference between Corey and my baby daddy. Corey always had me with him, like he was proud of what he had. I was his arm candy. He often called me his pretty young thang. That made me feel so special and amazing. My baby daddy was nothing like that. I had to admit, being wanted always felt good.

Ten minutes into our meal, my nigga's phone began to ring. Corey told us to sit tight and exited the building. The dude had arrived, and Corey went to make the exchange. Majesta went to get a to-go bag while I threw our trash away. She came back with a nice-size bag and collected the food we hadn't finished eating. She put everything into the bag.

We left the restaurant and headed to Majesta's grandma's Lincoln Town Car. Corey hadn't been able to get the bitch's truck for a couple of days. That had left us in a rut. We were always having to spend money to get a dope fiend rental, or we had to bargain with somebody to use their car. I had to admit, this hindered business a little, but we were still able to get around. We both hopped inside the ride and waited on Corey to finish handling business. A few minutes later, he got out of the connect's ride and leaped into the backseat of the Town Car.

"Baby," he said, puffing hard, like he was out of breath. "I got two hundred Lortabs, a bottle of Tussionex, and some dope."

I knew when we got to the house, I was going to have to cook up white stuff. I was ready to make some money, though. As we drove, Corey was on his phone, calling around to see if he could get us into another car.

"Why y'all can't get the truck?" Majesta whispered.

I shrugged my shoulders and rolled my eyes. Using that truck was good for us. I just hated that it belonged to her. It made me feel like I was doing something wrong by being in it. At the same time, Corey didn't seem to care. I was always in it, and sometimes, I even drove it. So I knew he couldn't have cared for her if he was doing the game like that.

When we arrived in Abilene, my homegirl dropped us off. Drew arrived at the same time we were letting ourselves into the crib. Drew and I headed into the kitchen. He helped me get started cooking the product. Corey used my brother's girlfriend's car to hit some licks across town, promising to return as soon as he could.

By the time Corey got back, Drew and I had just about all the dope cooked. I heard him tell my brother to take him to Tye to get a dope fiend rental. Then he came in and kissed me.

"I'm gonna leave to get us this car. I'll be back." Corey gave me a smooch and left.

While he was gone, I cleaned up the kitchen. I made sure to wipe all the crack residue off of everything on the counters, the utensils and the pot we had used, and the microwave. I also decided to do a little housekeeping. I cleaned the bathroom and took out the trash.

Corey came back and decided we were going to go out tonight to relax. He told me he was sleepy and was going to take a nap. While my baby was asleep, I made 150 dollars off of his phone for us. I kept the money in our stash, which helped us both calculate how much we had made back so far.

An hour and a half later, Corey got up, energized and ready for the night. He had called Bruce and Justine and had asked them to go out with us. Drew and his girl were beefin' with each other, like always, so we knew Drew's hands were tied for the night and they wouldn't be joining us. Nobody wanted to be around Koa when she was in a bad mood, anyway.

I decided to hop in the shower. I straightened my hair real quick. Since I hadn't done any laundry this week, I was forced to dress very casually. I decided to iron a white T-shirt and crease up my black Dickies. I was going to go relaxed tonight, toss back a few drinks, and enjoy some time with my man.

Before we headed out to the Pub, we all took pictures of each other. I knew we were going to have the best time of our lives that night. Or that was how I felt it should be. Corey decided to pay for everybody's way in, but Bruce insisted that he was going to buy our drinks.

Bruce found us a table right away. We all claimed our seats around it. Just then Corey received a text message. He read it and smiled hard at his screen.

"My little sister sent me a picture of my nieces," he announced.

I leaned in and took a look. All of a sudden, I saw a drink fly all over Corey, drenching his phone in the process.

Stunned, I jumped out of my seat and looked up. Dollie was standing there, screaming at the top of her lungs. She was pissed, and her little bitty voice was booming from rage. Her tiny, soft-spoken ass was lit up like a ferocious lion. I was stuck, not really sure how I was supposed to react. I was frozen in place.

I frantically looked around and saw that people had stopped what they were doing to watch. I tried to approach her to get her to lower her voice. She was mad, and on the cool, she should have known what was going on. There was no way no female would be that naive in this situation. Corey was never with her, was always in her truck, and was right there with me, where he belonged. I was somewhat surprised that it had taken her slow ass this long to figure out what was going on.

The bitch noticed me coming toward her, and she assumed a stance like she was going to fight me. She was enraged, was seething with anger, and her fists were clenched. She looked like she was ready to whup my ass. I froze in my tracks, and her fury sent a shiver down my spine. By then, everybody in the entire club was observing us. The security guards came rushing toward us. I backed up, in hopes of preventing any more drama.

Just then, Dollie and her redheaded friend stormed out of the building, with no assistance from security. Dollie had flipped over our table, causing our drinks to fall on the floor. Corey was staring at the door through which Dollie had exited. For a minute, I thought I saw a wave of sadness in his eyes. At just that moment, the authorities walked up to us and informed us that we had to leave. They were kicking us out of the club due to the confrontation.

"Fuck that! They started it! Why do *we* have to leave? Them hoes are already gone!" my sister protested.

"Ma'am, I'm not going to tell you again. Get the fuck out," the man yelled.

Bruce grabbed my sister's arm, and we all marched out to the parking lot.

"I guess that's it," I heard Corey mutter to himself.

We all got in the car, and then we headed toward my house in silence, which gave me time to think through my confusion. What the hell did Corey mean by that?

Chapter 21

"That bitch got me fucked up!" I heard Majesta yelling.

I quickly exited the bathroom. I walked into the living room. Corey and my brother, Drew, were watching TV. My sister's husband was in the kitchen with one of our partnas from the hood, Young Soljah, cutting up the rest of the coke they had just finished cooking. Majesta had just arrived at my house. She was so mad, her voice carried throughout the whole entire house.

"What you talkin' about, friend?" I said to her, approaching her cautiously.

She came over and hugged me. "Corey's stupid little ex-girlfriend," Majesta said.

The events from last night's fiasco were still replaying in my head. I hadn't had a chance to fill Majesta in on the stunt that little stuck-up bitch had pulled at the Pub. I had a feeling she had already heard about it. Why else would she be so mad?

I was really contemplating airing out my feelings about the way that nigga had left the club. That was my main concern right there. Had I imagined that he briefly appeared to feel some kind of way about her getting in our faces? What was that all about? Fuck that bitch and her crybaby fits. What was up with my nigga, though? Corey had said, and I quote, "I guess that's it." Was he really fucked up, or was that just a statement? I didn't think he intended for me to hear his comment. I'd be lying if I said it did not mean anything. It even had me second-guessing shit. One thing was for certain and two were for sure, she wasn't getting my man back.

"Say, big bro, roll a sweet up for me," Majesta told Corey.

Majesta sat down in the recliner. She motioned for me to sit down beside her. I did just that, as I was growing even more curious about what she was fixing to say next.

"Word on the street is, Dollie wants to see you." She pulled out a cigarette from her Marlboro box. "I ain't gonna let her fuck with you, though."

I burst out laughing. Was this girl serious? Obviously, Corey didn't want this girl. Despite the fact that my mind was going a hundred miles an hour because of his comment, I told myself to look at the facts. He lived with me, he bought me things, and we were always together. Always. That was something nobody could even deny. Just knowing this made it easier for me to erase from my head that remark he'd made.

"I don't get it. She should know by now. Why the fuck is this broad acting all surprised?" I said.

I looked over at Corey. He shook his head. He looked like he was lost in thought. I watched as he finished rolling his sweet. His cell phone started ringing. He gestured for me to grab his phone. Obediently, I answered.

"Is this Ten?" a voice boomed out at me.

"Yeah, this me. What's good?" I said.

"I need an eight ball," the voice replied.

I went into the kitchen and looked in the cabinet closest to the refrigerator, where Corey kept the work. I took out everything I needed and began to cut the dope up. I stopped when I had the amount the caller was asking for.

"Who's this?" I asked when I was finished.

"It's Kitty from around the corner," the voice answered.

Now it became clear to me. I let Corey know what was up once I ended the call. Immediately, the phone started to ring again. *Showtime*, I thought to myself. I signaled to Majesta to start taking phone calls for us.

"Baby, is it time?" a voice whispered in my ear.

I turned around to find my sexy boyfriend standing behind me with his sweet in his mouth. I removed it from his lips and kissed him gently. I nodded my head.

"Let's get it, then," he said.

Corey turned around and began barking orders at Bruce and Young Soljah. My brother entered the kitchen. He joined in their conversation.

I walked back over to where Majesta was sitting. She looked up at me and stated that Dandy and Fred, two of our loyal customers, both wanted a fifty piece. Suzy had called also. She was looking for a dub. I returned to the kitchen and began to cut up the dope some more. After I was finished with that, Corey got dressed, and then we all loaded into the car. Majesta stayed behind to watch Karen and Ty for me.

Before we pulled out of the driveway, Corey patted his pockets and started asking where his phone was. Bruce and Young Soljah both stated that they didn't have it.

"I think you left it on the kitchen table, bro," Drew said.

"I'll get it, baby." I hopped out of the car and ran inside to get Corey's phone. Right when I grabbed it, it began to ring, and I saw a private number come up on the screen. I immediately answered.

"What you need?" I stated into the phone.

"Bitch, where Corey at?"

I paused for a few seconds, filled with shock. The cell phone was glued to my hand. I mean, she was just flipping tables and shit last night, trying to square up over a nigga who clearly didn't want her ass anymore. Now she was calling the very next day? What the fuck for? This ho had the audacity to hit his fuckin' line now?

Disgusted, I shook my head back and forth. This girl was so stupid. Could she not see he didn't want her ass?

"Girl, what do you want?" I said as I headed down the hall to look for Majesta.

"I asked to speak to Corey, not you."

"Didn't you embarrass yourself enough? He ain't checking for you, bitch, so, again, what do you want?"

The evil sound of her laughter filled my ears. I wanted to hang up on her ass. What she said next caused my heart to drop.

"Embarrass myself, huh? Your so-called man been calling me nonstop. I want to know what he wants."

I stopped. So maybe what I was worried about was true, then. He was really feeling some kind of way that shit had gone down the way it had. I knew something wasn't right when I heard him say that shit! But fuck that. I was not letting him go without a fight.

"He don't want your ass!" I yelled at her angrily, not caring if my emotions showed through the earpiece.

I heard this ho take a deep breath, like she was fixing to go off on ya girl, right? I took the phone from my ear and handed it right on over to Majesta for her to finish this ugly-ass bitch off. I wasn't going to argue with her. It was a waste of time and money. Majesta ended the call after a series of curse words and insults were hurled back and forth between the two, and then she gave me the phone, and we both started laughing. After all, she was the one who was making herself look dumb. The phone rang again. It was a private call. I answered it, and who was on the other end but Dollie.

"Don't you get it?" I shouted into the phone. "He's with me now, not you. Quit calling my nigga's phone!"

Chapter 22

Dollie

When I got up this morning, I was still in a daze, due to all the things going on. I didn't remember anything I did prior to arriving at work. I didn't remember fixing my hair. I didn't remember getting Drake ready to go to day care with my aunt, let alone what I chose for him to wear today. I didn't know how I even managed to get dressed. I still arrived at work on time. The one thing I couldn't do was smile. What the fuck was this ho-ass nigga doing to me?

My boss immediately noticed my frazzled look. He sensed something was wrong.

"Doll?" he said, his face filled with concern. "Are you all right, hun?"

I think I am, I thought to myself as I took my position behind my desk.

"I'm all right, Jerry," I choked out.

He knew I was full of shit. "Maybe you should take the day off—" he began, but I cut him off.

"Jerry, I feel great. The last thing I need is to be at home." I spoke carefully to him, trying not to let my emotions show. "Just let me stay. If I am not up to par with my performance, I'll go home."

He accepted my plea bargain and handed me some files to put away and a list of clients I had to call either about making a payment or setting up an appointment.

After he finished giving me his schedule for the day, he grabbed a cup of coffee and rushed into his office to meet with his nine o' clock appointment.

As I began to get into my routine for the day, Tammy waltzed in, carrying her book bag and a change of clothes. I chuckled to myself. She was always in a hurry. But she'd never leave her home without her Gucci collection. She disappeared in the back, and moments later, she reemerged. She had pulled her hair into a bun, and she now sported a nice white blouse and black dress pants. She had on some black Coach slip-on shoes and matching glasses.

"Jerry has court today?" she asked as she sat at her desk, which was kitty-corner to mine.

"Not until one," I replied. "He has you down to go with him at one and then to go talk to a potential client at the county jail around four thirty today."

She rolled her eyes. She started rummaging around her desk, and after she got settled, she quietly waited for me to finish making a couple of calls. Once she saw I was through, she opened her big-ass mouth.

"You look bad."

"Thanks." I glanced at myself in the mirror I kept in a desk drawer. My eyes were still kind of puffy, and I hadn't even bothered to comb the tangles out of my long hair before putting it in a ponytail. I hadn't even put on makeup. Hell, I hadn't even applied any lotion. I quickly grabbed my Jergens lotion bottle from a desk drawer and squirted some in my hands.

"You're going to need more than that," she sang out, laughing at me.

I rolled my eyes, and she quickly wiped that grin off her face. She grabbed her water bottle, walked over, and sat on the edge of my desk.

"What happened now?" she asked before she took a sip.

"He's been cheating on me," I said to her. "He's been dogging me out for that trash, Tenosha, this whole entire time."

"Oh, girl—" she began, but I cut her off.

"Why is he doing this to me!" I had raised my voice, and the tears had started flowing again. "I kept money on his books. I went to go see him religiously . . . every weekend. I did that. I did all of that, and he gets out and treats me like this?"

Tammy grabbed a Kleenex from the box on my desk and wiped the tears off my face. "You can do a whole lot better than Corey." She put some lotion on her hands and rubbed it into my face. "You don't need him. He needed you. You have a beautiful son. You're gorgeous. You got a real nice truck and a very decent job. If he wants to settle for less, let him. If you ask me, he settled for somebody who was more on his level. You were way out of his league, girl. Don't bring yourself down for that convict."

She was right.

She rose from her perch on my desk, walked behind me, combed her fingers through my hair, and fixed my very sloppy ponytail. After she finished up with my hair, she did my filing for me, giving me time to pull myself together again. Then she squeezed my shoulder. I immediately snapped back and started making phone calls again.

She was right about everything. I *was* better than Corey. So, how did I let my heart understand that so I could let him go?

Chapter 23

After I left work, I stopped by my aunt's day care to pick up Drake. We headed to Baskin-Robbins for some ice cream and then went home. When we arrived, no one was there, of course. My uncle had left a note saying he was going to have to close the bakery again and telling my aunt to come up there if she wanted to. I put *Lilo & Stitch* on for Drake and decided to prepare some chili.

About halfway through my preparations, the phone rang.

"Hello?" I said.

"What's up?" an unfamiliar voice said.

I hurriedly lifted the lid on the chili pot and stirred a couple of times. "Uncle Justin and Aunt Audrina ain't here," I stated. "May I ask who's calling?" I grabbed a pen and a sheet of paper from the counter and prepared myself to write.

"I ain't calling for them, but you can tell them I said hello," the voice said softly.

My face started to get hot, and for a brief moment, a wave of confusion consumed me. I really did not feel like playing with this person right now.

"Who are you calling for, then?" I asked in a monotone.

The caller took a deep breath. "It's me, Drew," he said softly. "I was just calling to make sure you were okay."

"I'm all right," I replied flatly and slammed the phone down.

I wasn't okay. I felt humiliated, dumb, and very unattractive. How could you go on, knowing that the person you were in love with had played you like a PlayStation?

Just then, my aunt Audrina walked in the kitchen.

"Mmm, mmm, mmm. That smells delicious!" She smiled as she looked in the pot to see what was cooking.

She walked into the living room and scooped up my son.

"Are you all right?" she asked me when she came back into the kitchen. She placed my son in his big boy seat at the table and gave him a toy train that was on the kitchen counter.

"I believe this chili is about done," she said as she grabbed the corn bread mix out of the cabinet and a couple of eggs and the milk from the fridge. She took out a bowl and the mixer. "I'll pop us some corn bread out, and we'll be good to go."

She sang as she preheated the oven, mixed everything together, poured the batter into a square-shaped baking pan, and placed the pan in the oven. She had already seen my uncle's note, so she grabbed a carryout plate and bowls so she could take some food over to him later.

She fixed her eyes on me. "You never answered my question. Are you okay?"

"No," I whispered. I was sitting at the kitchen table now.

My aunt Audrina sat down across from me. I told her everything that had happened between me and my ex. I talked and cried. She sat there patiently and listened. After I had finally finished talking, she got up and removed her corn bread from the oven. She put some corn bread on plates for Drake and me and ladled chili into a bowl for me and brought them over to us. Drake was still too young to appreciate chili.

"Everybody plays a fool, Doll," she began. "I can tell you all day you are worth more than that, but do you believe that?" She took Drake's toy from him so he could concentrate on eating his food. Then she walked over to the stove.

I shook my head no. My proud self was at an all-time low, and for what reason, I did not know. All I knew was that I had hatred inside of me, and my heart felt like fifty million bricks were being thrown at it. I was literally all fucked up inside.

"Dollie, you can do better than that," my aunt stated, ladling chili into one of the carryout bowls for herself. "Don't let a man get the best of you, especially somebody like that. Trust me, honey. When his water runs dry, he'll be back. But you got to decide if you're going to take him and his bullshit back. Let that drama go. He wasn't ready to change, and the longer you stick with him, the worse he'll make you look. You're the prize, honey. He never was."

"That's so much easier said than done, Audrina," I choked out, the tears welling up inside again. "I feel like I am all alone and nobody understands me. I wish somebody would tell me what I did to deserve this."

My aunt sat down beside me and rubbed the back of my neck as I broke down once again and cried. When I was finally through crying, I wiped my nose on my napkin. I walked over to the sink to wash my face and hands.

Drake looked at me and then back at my aunt. "She done yet?" he said. "I hungry. Her crying get on my nerves."

My aunt and I looked at each other and burst out laughing. I walked over to my handsome three-year-old and kissed his forehead to give him the okay to eat.

I sat across from him and dug into my bowl. My aunt ladled some chili into the carryout bowl for my uncle and then placed two squares of corn bread on the carryout plate. Then she placed their food in a plastic grocery sack.

"Doll, I'm about to go to the shop and help your uncle out for a bit. Get yourself some rest and remember this. God don't like ugly, and that boy will reap what he sows." She grabbed her food and headed toward the front door.

Chapter 24

Even though it was a Saturday night, I had decided not to go out with the girls. I had had a long workweek, and now I had my aunt and uncle's house all to myself. My son had left for the weekend with his grandma. My uncle Justin and my aunt Audrina had left for the weekend to visit one of their kids in Austin. The only thing I had to do was go check on the bakery from time to time. All I knew was this was the time for me to get my head together.

I was curled up on my uncle's fluffy mauve couch, about to rent a couple of movies. I had changed out of my clothes right after Drake left. I was wearing my pink-and-white flannel pajamas. I had braided my hair into one long French braid that went neatly down my back. I had my Mickey Mouse slippers on. Nearby, I had the remote control to the television and the DVD player, my bowl of popcorn, and the cordless phone. I was good to go.

My mind was starting to get clear about the whole thing with Ten and Corey. I should have seen it coming, but I hadn't. Or maybe I had seen it, but I had just refused to see. I had wanted so badly for things to work out between us that I'd overlooked the signs. All I knew was that my heart was in pain and my mind was in a very bitter place.

Corey hadn't called all week, and that hurt me. Really, it should simply let me know that was where he wanted to be. I shouldn't be upset or mad about it all. I should just make peace with it. The one thing I had a hard time battling was the idea of being used. *Who would use somebody like that? Why the fuck waste my time? Be a man, and do what you need to do without hurting somebody else in the process.*

I had begun to watch one of my favorite childhood movies *Crooklyn*, when I heard a knock at the door. At first I didn't want to get up and answer the door. I was focused on healing myself. I'd been wallowing in my own misery privately, by myself, and this person had the nerve to disrupt it. The knocking sounds persisted.

Who is this? I thought to myself.

I went to the window and peeped out. Drew was standing there, looking fresh to death in his blue-and-white Gucci shirt and fresh Robin's jeans. He even had on all white Air Force Ones. Shaking the image of Drew's freshly shaven face and faded haircut, I was determined to be as rude as I possibly could be. It was going to be hard to do because he was so damn fine.

I stomped to the front door, swung it open, and placed my hands firmly on my hips. It wasn't hard to be mad. I was embarrassed, hurt, and angry. I had so many fucking questions going through my head. I looked like a fuckin' crash dummy because that idiot had played me like a fiddle. The whole damn neighborhood had known about this shit and had taken turns pulling on my strings. I was fucked up about it all.

"How are you, Dollie?" he asked me. The expression on his face was soothing.

"I'm fine, Drew," I said.

I positioned my body in front of the door so he couldn't enter the house. Seeing the stance I had taken, he stepped back. He began to look uncomfortable and uncertain.

"I just wanted to stop by and check on you and your son," he said. "I haven't seen you guys around anywhere. I thought I'd come by and see how you were doing."

I rolled my eyes at him. *Is this fool for real right now?* "Drake is good. I'm good," I replied dryly.

Drew looked at me as if he was going to say something else. Instead he nodded his head and then waved good-bye as he headed across the porch.

"Drew!" I called out to him.

He turned around and faced me.

"Why would you see me anywhere after the way your sister and your newfound brother-in-law disrespected me?"

Drew looked at me in surprise.

Before he could answer, I continued. "I was your friend. At least, I thought I was, and you let that shit happen. You might as well have played me for a fool too. I'd appreciate it if you never came by here again." I slammed the door in his face.

What the fuck, man? This was beginning to get the best of me, yet at the same time, it felt good to say that shit. True enough, I had said that shit to the wrong person. His ho-ass friend should have been man enough to let me say those things to his face, but that would never happen. I also felt like a negative reaction was what these people wanted out of me. I was going to do the total opposite. It was time for me to do me.

I paced back and forth in the living room as my thoughts scrambled together. Me trying to get back at them would be too childish. Plus, if I did that, she would know she had won. But what did this bitch win besides a convicted felon? He really wasn't a prize. No, not at all.

I chewed on my bottom lip as I felt a new sense of myself rush through me. First off, I could cut my hair off and turn over a new leaf. I could go to see my beautician, and then I could get that bob haircut I'd been wanting. A huge smile was spreading across my face.

What else could I do? I sat down on the couch and began absentmindedly flipping through the newspapers.

I went to the classified section, and I stopped to look through the ads. It was nice staying with my aunt and uncle, but I wanted my own place again. Then it hit me. I didn't have that extra burden anymore. The dead weight had been released from my shoulders. What could Corey do for me? Not a damn thang, but give me a fuckin' migraine, and I was tired of them. I was going to do this for me and my child, and for my own peace of mind. The only place I could go from here was up.

Ecstatic about the new decisions I had made, I called my cousin at the bakery. When Victoria answered the phone, I didn't even say hello. I just rushed into what I was going to do.

"Whoa, whoa. Slow down, girl," Vic commanded. "Now, tell me this. You are going to cut your hair?"

"Yes, ma'am," I said proudly. "It's a meaningful cut. It'll symbolize letting go of dead weight."

"You cutting your hair is a symbol?" I heard her say. "Go to sleep, child. You'll forget about it in the morning."

I rolled my eyes. She thought I was playing, but I was dead serious. "I really want to do this, Vic. I have to do something for me."

Victoria placed me on hold for a few minutes, and when she came back on the line, she stated, "I think it's a great idea. I'm proud of you for making changes for your-self, and not in the favor of a loser who never deserved anybody like you to begin with. I'm glad you're back, Doll. Knock them trashy hoes and sorry-ass niggas dead!"

Chapter 25

Tenosha

As the day finally slowed down and the licks stopped coming in, Corey, the boys, and I headed back to the house. Majesta had left, but my sister was at the house with my kids. Corey, Bruce, Drew, and Young Soljah went into the kitchen to count up the money.

Justine and I sat on the couch and told each other about our day. Right when we were finishing up, Corey came over and sat beside me.

"I'm going to take Drew to get his girl's car. Then I'm gonna drop Young Soljah off in the hood. Me and Bruce will be back," he announced.

"Let's take the rental we got and leave y'all car here," Bruce said as he took the keys from Justine. He kissed his young wife on the forehead.

Corey handed the keys over to me. "I got my phone with me. I took some dope too. Go on ahead and clean that kitchen up from earlier," he instructed.

"I will, babe," I said. I got up and headed to the kitchen.

As I cleaned up in there, Justine hooked my living room up for me. Once I was done, I got my two youngest ready for bed. My sister helped Hanson with his homework. She gave him and Marie a bath after they were through looking over his work. After she finished with them, I put them to bed.

Justine and I posted up outside, on the front porch, and I began to tell her about the phone call from Dollie and how I went off on her.

"Damn!" She chuckled to herself, raising her hand to her lips as she laughed. "The whole damn situation is fucked up, though."

I nodded in agreement. "But, shit, Corey is mine now, and nobody else's. She better quit playin' and stop callin' his phone."

"Why would she think they were together, though?" Justine wondered aloud.

"Who gives a damn?" I replied.

I then pulled out my cell to hit my nigga up. He told me he was on his way back. I hung up and looked over at my sister.

One day down and many more to come, I thought.

A couple of days later, Corey and I were back on the highway. We had begun to run low on cocaine, and we were on our way to meet another connect in Eastland, once again.

I had arranged for one of our customers to come over to the house and get the kids off to school so I could ride with my man. At 4:30 a.m. sharp, the dope fiend had arrived at the house, and Corey and I had headed out. We had just gotten a rental car from Avis the night before. It had become too much of a hassle to use some lady's car. We had planned to go this early in the morning because Corey had to report to his parole officer at 9:00 a.m. I was also going to start looking for a job this morning, like we had discussed the night before.

As we drove to Eastland, Corey talked to me about his sister and brother. They were both coming down here to see him this weekend. I was excited to meet them.

"I haven't seen Tiger in a long time," Corey said as he twisted up a sweet. "Tiger and his girl have two little girls together. Cola and Candace. I remember Cola, but I have never met Candace before."

I listened to my man as he spoke graciously. His deep baritone voice was even lower when he spoke about his family. The deepness of his voice was soothing enough to put a baby to sleep. I wished right then that we were at home in bed, talking about it, so I could feel the vibrations of his voice as I rested my head against his chest. But we weren't at home, and I was driving, so I had to keep my focus and concentrate.

I also loved the way his forehead moved when he smiled. That was my baby. He finished rolling up his sweet and placed it under the visor for later.

"You'll love Naomi. That's my nigga," he said as he faced me. "She has a two-year-old daughter named Nestle. My mom ain't coming down this time, but I will take you to meet her later." He turned on the radio and leaned back in his seat as I focused my attention on the road.

Thirty minutes later, we pulled into the Taco Bell parking lot. Goose arrived ten minutes later. He was an older white male, very clean cut, but he had a slick-ass mouth. You could tell he was a hustler, if you were in that field of work, when he opened his mouth to talk. He was smart as hell, though. From what I understood, that man had been hustling for years and ain't been caught yet! At least, that was the way he told it.

Goose approached our car, sporting a badass Vikings jersey and some white shoes. I couldn't tell what brand he had on, because his pants hung so low over them. His sandy-blond hair was pulled back into a tight, neatly combed ponytail that reached halfway down his back. His black shades hid his eyes and stood out against his pale white skin. He was pretty fly for a white guy.

He hopped out of his Cadillac truck and slid into the backseat of our Camry. I handed him the money, and he quickly counted it all to himself. He handed Corey a big-ass ziplock bag full of Ecstasy pills, a bottle of Tussionex, and a big Crown Royal bag full of cocaine. Then Goose got out of the car and headed toward the Taco Bell entrance. We pulled out of the parking lot and headed back toward Abilene.

"I smell money!" Corey sang as he lit up his sweet.

Shit. I did too.

Chapter 26

By Thursday night, we had sold out of everything we had. Corey had to go and re-up a little bit with one of his big homies until we could meet Goose again the next morning. Corey decided we would go after we took the oldest two to school and dropped the other two off at their dad's parents.

When we left this time, Bruce and Justine rode along. We had the same rental car, and when we got back, I was going to call the rental car agency and have them extend our lease for another week.

"Man, those XOs were on point," Corey said to Bruce as I drove along.

Bruce agreed with him.

"I hope he has the same ones. Everybody ate them hoes up," Justine said, chiming in.

Justine and Bruce were looking to get a couple of pounds of Reggie and a bag of Ecstasy themselves. This time, we were getting two bags of pills, and our connect was giving us a good deal on an ounce of coke.

"I gotta get ready for my brother and sister to come in this weekend," Corey said.

"Naomi and Tiger?" Bruce asked. Bruce began telling Justine about Corey's brother and sister.

"You want some new Js?" Corey asked me.

I nodded my head yes, trying to contain my excitement.

"You know, I'm going to be looking all right. I need baby to be on point too," Corey said.

We pulled up to a McDonald's, which was the meeting spot this time. Goose pulled up ten minutes later. Justine got out of the car and went inside the restaurant to order some drinks. While she was inside, Goose slid into the backseat, a blunt in his hand. I could smell a mixture of Sean John's I Am King cologne and marijuana coming from him. He took a hit of his blunt and passed it to Bruce. They all made the exchange as they passed the blunt around. Goose got out of the car once the blunt was completely gone and headed inside the McDonald's. A minute later, Justine came out with four drinks in a cup holder.

We drove back to the house. When we arrived back home, we all got out of the car. Bruce and Corey immediately headed into the kitchen, and a half hour later they left in the rental to hit the block. Justine was taking me to a job interview, so she stayed behind. I had a job interview at Jack in the Box at 1:45 p.m. It was already 11:30 a.m., so I began to get ready.

After I got dressed, flatironed my hair, and braided it neatly into one long French braid, Majesta arrived at my house. She had agreed to pick up Hanson and Marie from school for me today and to care for them until I got home. Later I would take them to their daddy's.

When I walked out of my bedroom, Majesta took a picture of me. "You are so beautiful!" she cooed at me. "I love it when you flatiron your hair."

Soon Justine and I left the house. We arrived at the Jack in the Box at 1:30 p.m. I went inside, while my sister waited for me in the car. I was finished with my interview at 2:15 p.m. When I walked out, I knew that I had been hired for the position they needed to fill.

Justine took me by the HUD and food stamp office so I could report that I had a job. Then we headed to my house, and when we pulled up, I saw that my man had already made it back with some of the homies.

I went inside and slipped into something comfortable. I put on my black capris, a white T-shirt, and my black-and-white Air Maxs. I heard Corey telling Justine that Majesta was keeping my older kids overnight at her grandma's house for us. My baby daddy's parents were still looking after the youngest two.

Corey ushered me into the kitchen, and we both started cooking the dope up. He had already sold a little bit of the dope, and the pills were going fast. Goose was coming through Abilene tomorrow and had already agreed to meet us so we could re-up on that. We stayed in the kitchen for damn near an hour, cooking the dope. By the time we were finished, my sister and her husband had already left, but the homies were still at the house. Before we got ready to go do some work, I told Corey about my new job. He gave me the biggest hug and the longest kiss.

"I'm proud of you," he whispered in my ear. "Baby, we need that. Real talk. Now the police won't be looking at us so much."

As we got ready to depart, Corey cleared the house out and paid the next-door neighbor forty dollars to clean up the kitchen, bathroom, and living room. I could get used to this.

Chapter 27

Saturday finally rolled around. My kids were still with Majesta and my baby daddy's parents. Corey had given Majesta a hundred dollars to keep the oldest two through Sunday. I was glad he had done that. Hell, I was even happier that she had agreed to do this for us. She was what I called the true definition of a real friend. She was always there to help and to ride for us when we needed her to. I was feeling even more grateful for her because we had ended up having a big-ass party the night before at the house. I needed all the sleep I could get after that.

When I finally woke up, I lay around in bed. I was really afraid to see how bad the house looked. Plus, all that Keystone Light and UV Vodka I had drunk was kicking my ass. I rolled over onto my left side. Corey was sound asleep and was snoring loudly. All that X he had taken and all those drinks he had sipped on had him knocked out on his ass. I covered up his naked body and got out of bed. I covered up my own body with an oversize flannel shirt and walked out into the hallway.

I silently closed the bedroom door behind me and inspected the hallway. It looked decent to me. I peeped into my kids' rooms. A few weeks ago, I had rearranged the rooms so that the girls now shared a room and the boys did too. When I peeped into Hanson and Ty's room, you could tell it hadn't been disturbed at all. But Karen and Marie's room was a different story. Their room had the faint smell of cigarette, Black & Mild, and weed smoke, so I knew people had been chillin' in there. Karen's bed was all messed up, so I knew somebody had had sex on her bed.

I closed their door and examined the bathroom that was across the hall from their room. People had been in there as well. There was powder residue on the counter-top. The toilet paper was all gone, and there were beer bottles, food, and a couple of condom wrappers all over the floor. I closed that door and headed toward the living room.

My big bros Blue and Jorge were passed out on the floor in front of the TV. All night long they must have played the Nintendo Wii that Corey had got from a dope fiend two days ago. The TV was still on. Both of them had a controller clutched tightly in their hands. I shook my head in amusement. I tiptoed silently over to the television and turned it off.

I continued to inspect the living room. A bottle of rum was sitting on the coffee table. Blunts and ashes completely covered it, along with some empty bottles of codeine and Tuss. My little brother, Drew, was asleep on the couch. I shook my head at him as well. Koa and my brother had been arguing a lot lately. This was for sure going to spark another fight between the two of them.

I just hoped her ass didn't come over here with that unnecessary drama. I couldn't help but think this. My poor little brother was not happy with that psycho girl. I saw his phone on the floor, and I crept up to it to take a look at it. Eighteen missed calls, ten voice messages, and I knew all of them were from his crazy-ass girlfriend. At that moment his phone lit up again. I decided to take one for the team and answer. I prepared myself to defend my brother as I quickly walked into the hallway, away from the sleeping boys.

"Hello?"

"Who the fuck is this? Where the fuck is Drew at? Bitch, you fucking my man?" I shook my head in disgust as this crazy-ass female kept barking questions and making dry-ass threats. I knew Koa's ass was not about to bust a muthafuckin' grape. I tolerated my headache, which was beginning to grow by the minute, as she continued on with her bitching.

"Koa, it's me, Tenosha. Drew is over here at my house, sound asleep."

"Oh! I didn't recognize your voice. Can you wake him up for me?"

I was not about to disturb my brother so she could yell at him and give him the third degree. I couldn't stand this girl. I loathed the fact that she had made it her mission to make his life miserable. I just wished he would leave that ho alone.

"Koa, my grandma and all of them are over here. Can I have him hit you back as soon as they leave?"

"Yeah, that's cool."

"Thanks, Mama." I hung up my brother's phone. I put it back where I had got it, making sure to be quiet and not to wake anybody up.

I then headed over to the foyer window to take a quick look at my front yard. The rental was in the driveway, Blue's Cadillac was behind it, and Jorge's Lincoln was parked in the yard. I walked into the kitchen. Pizza boxes were sprawled all over the kitchen counters and the table, and they were blocking the path to the back door and the garage door. Dirty dishes were piled up in the sink, and the trash can was overflowing with empty cigarette boxes, Keystone Light cans, Miller Lite bottles, and Bud Ice forty-ounce bottles.

I wished silently to myself that Corey could get somebody to clean this up. I didn't want any parts of having to make this house look like a train had not run through it.

I decided to go on ahead and straighten up the kitchen. I was going to have to restore order in the kids' bathroom as well.

I was winding up my task in the bathroom when I took a peek into my bedroom to steal a look at my man. He was still in a deep slumber. After I finished cleaning the kids' bathroom, I turned to the task of making myself presentable. I jumped in the shower and shampooed my hair. I was determined to look super fly today. Seeing that Corey was still trying to contact that bitch, despite the fact that he was with me, bothered me. After she showed her ass, he had tried to contact her. I opted against discussing the whole matter with him. I was going to step my game up and show him just why I was the best choice for him. We belonged together.

Today was going to be special due to the fact this was the first time I was going to meet his people. It was required that I look and dress my best. I put some mousse in my hands and ran them through my ringlets. Then I put on a pink tank top and some blue jean shorts. I also put on my new pink Air Force Ones, which Corey had gotten for me yesterday for the get-together we had last night.

I glanced at the clock. It was already noon, and I knew it was going to be a minute before Corey got up. When I walked back up front, I noticed that Blue and Jorge had left while I was showering. My brother, Drew, was up and was arguing with his bitch over the phone. I sat beside him on the couch and pretended like I was watching the TV. He continued to argue with his girl. When he was done, he asked me to take him home. I grabbed the keys, and we got into the car. As I turned out of the neighborhood, Drew and I began to talk.

"What's up with you and Koa?" I asked him casually, trying not to sound too nosy.

Drew shrugged his shoulders and stared ahead for a minute before he replied. "I don't think I will be dealing with her for too much longer. She taking a nigga for granted, for real. Can't take this bullshit anymore."

"How's that?"

"What you mean, how's that?" Drew replied, sounding a bit irritated.

"How is she taking you for granted, little brother?" I turned the radio off, giving him my undivided attention.

My brother normally kept shit to himself. When something was bothering him, he usually would come to me for advice. I didn't know why exactly, but it was probably because he felt more comfortable discussing his deep personal business with me over everybody else. He wanted to get some things off his chest now. I could tell. I wanted to make sure he did what was best for him. More importantly, I want my brother to realize that I would be here eternally for him, no matter what. Even if he basically wanted me just to listen to him, I was all ears.

"'Cause, man, she doesn't appreciate shit. It be the little shit she does that pisses me the hell off. She be accusing me of cheating and shit, but the truth is, I think that ho is fuckin' around on me. Now her conscience is troubling her. She chased me around the house with a damn hammer the other night."

The frustration in my brother's voice tugged at my heart a little. I didn't like hearing that he was so unhappy. The fact that she was trying to harm him made me angry. He should have told Justine and me when it first happened. We didn't play when it came to him. Period.

"So, what are you going to do about it, Drew?"

"I'm gonna leave. Real soon, because I can't deal with that shit. Plus, she really starts to act stupid when y'all sell her them damn pills. Y'all need to stop that shit, at least until I can get the hell out of there."

"Damn, bro. I had no idea that those pills resulted in her wanting to get to trippin' like that. I will let Corey know."

"That nigga already knows! He witnessed it plenty of times. Stop selling her that shit!" he demanded.

I tried to digest that declaration for a little bit. Then I spoke up again. "If you're not happy, bro, just leave. I would hate for anything horrible to happen to you."

"Listen, sis, I got this. Plus, I got my eye on somebody else."

That caught my ears. "Who?" I quizzed him.

"Don't worry about that. Just know that I'm going to end things first with Koa before I get at this chick. She's a lady, and I got to come to her correct." He looked out the window from the passenger side. "Do not sell my girl any more pills until I leave her ass! Make sure you tell Corey too."

"Will do."

We rode for a little bit in complete silence. I was waiting for him to finish talking before I turned on the radio. I had a feeling he was not done talking yet.

"Say, sis," he began again. "We've known Corey for a minute now. I know you like him and all, but you need to watch that man."

"Oh, Drew," I sighed.

His request made me stop wondering about this mystery girl, and at the same time, I brushed off his warning. Drew had never stopped trying to shield me and Justine. We were his *big* sisters, and yet he defended us like a pit bull. I began to giggle to myself.

"Don't trip, little brother. I like Corey. He's so much different than Bobbie."

Drew shook his head. "I hope you know what you are doing. When you got with him, he had a girl. What makes you think he won't do it to you too?"

Good question, I thought to myself. "He is too good to me, that's why."

"Don't be stupid about this, Ten. Really look at the situation you got yourself into before you get even more deeply involved. I'm a nigga. If I'm speaking to you about it, it's because I know what's up. I can see the play. I just don't want you and your kids to get caught up in a web that can easily be avoided."

"That's your homeboy, though."

"Exactly."

I agreed to think about it even more before I got too serious with him. Again, I knew my brother meant well. But I was a big girl; I could hold my own. In addition, it was too late. My heart was already heavily invested in this man.

I dropped Drew off at his apartment. I stayed outside for a little bit to make sure everything was good before I drove off. I headed to the convenience store. I bought some candy and sodas to take to my kids. I put gas in my car. Then I drove by Majesta's. I sat over there for a bit, filling her in on everything that happened last night. I communicated with my children for a minute by phone before I traveled back to my house.

When I entered the house, I heard the shower running. Corey was awake. I sat on the couch and waited patiently for him to finish bathing. When he was finally done getting ready, he entered the living room and joined me on the couch.

"Damn!" he exclaimed. "This house is a mess. You didn't get this mess cleaned up before you left?" he joked. He narrowed his eyes at everything as he took a look around. Then he came over and kissed my lips. I put my hands on my hips once we broke the embrace.

"Boy, you should have seen the damn kitchen and bathroom," I said, defending myself. I filled him in on

Koa and Drew while he continued to scrutinize the mess around us.

"Damn. That's crazy. He needs to leave that bitch!" he said, sounding a bit distracted.

"Don't sell her no more pills, either," I challenged.

"I won't," he agreed, shaking his head.

I was able to get a good look at him. He looked nicely put together. He was decked out in a pair of True Religion jeans, a flannel shirt, and the white Jordans he got yesterday. He had topped off his outfit with a black-and-white New York hat. He had cleaned his face up nicely, shaving off the beard he had started to grow. I loved his clean-cut look. He must have liked my outfit too. His smiling eyes gave it away as he checked me out.

"We'll get somebody to tidy up this mess," he suggested, getting up off the couch. The keys were lying on the coffee table. He snatched them up. He grabbed both of my hands, then pulled me up off the couch.

"Let's go meet my family for lunch," he said.

Chapter 28

Over the next couple of weeks, I began to form a relationship with Corey's little sister. Tiger didn't seem to be that fond of me, although he was very polite. I was determined to change his opinion about me, though. I was going to be Tiger's favorite sister-in-law. I enjoyed being around Corey's family. For me to be accepted by them meant everything to me. Since Corey's mom didn't get a chance to visit us, we decided to go up there at some point with the kids so that I could meet her.

Corey and I had already turned in our rental car. We had found another smoker who agreed to loan out his car, so we hopped on that chance before anybody else did. This guy had a black Expedition and did not trip as long as we kept his ass geeked up. Corey had given him enough dope to last him until Tuesday, when he had to go to work. This setup was acceptable to us. It meant that we could take that trip out of town as planned.

That Friday, after Hanson and Marie got out of school, we picked up Ty and Karen from my mom's house. Then we got on the freeway and left Abilene. We cruised down I-20 East toward Dallas–Fort Worth. Corey had told me a little about his parents, and of course, I had already met his dad and his grandma.

A couple of hours later, we pulled in front of Corey's mom's house. Naomi and her little girl were already there.

"Corey!" Naomi screamed dramatically. She ran toward the SUV. When he opened the car door, she was there waiting for her big brother to give her a hug.

A shorter while later, a petite, tall white lady with red hair came out of the house, with a huge smile plastered across her face. Corey strolled over to her and gave her a hug, then kissed her cheek lightly. He had a big grin on his face that was identical to hers.

"Glad you haven't vanished back to jail yet," she kidded him.

I stood back, watching the scene unfold before me. Corey and his mom chatted for a few minutes. He seized his mom's hand and walked her over to us.

"Mom, I want you to meet my girl, Tenosha. These are her kids, Hanson, Marie, Tyrese, and Karen."

"How old are you?" she asked, laughing as she hugged and kissed my kids.

I was slightly taken aback by her questioning my age, though I knew I looked younger than I was, but then a wave of excitement swept through my body. I greeted his mom, laughing off her remark. We walked into the house, and the kids immediately took to Nestle. I held on to Karen, who was just beginning to walk well, and all the other kids ran out to the backyard to play.

Corey went into the kitchen to catch up with his mom. She was preparing supper. Naomi helped me unload the Expedition. We carried our bags to the bedrooms Corey's mom was having us stay in while we were here.

"I am so glad you are with my brother," Naomi stated. She helped me put our belongings away.

"Me too," I said. "You have no idea. My baby daddy wasn't all that great to me."

She immediately became concerned. I gave her a short version of my estranged relationship with my kids' father. By the time I was done, she was hugging me so hard, a bitch couldn't even breathe.

"Corey treats me like a queen." I beamed.

"He better!" She laughed. "I'll beat his ass."

Naomi and I sat on the bed. We snickered like two old-time girlfriends. We talked briefly about their childhood.

"So, you've been knowing my brother?" she asked.

I nodded my head.

"Why are ya'll just now getting together?" she quizzed.

"I wrote him while he was locked up here and there. But he really got at me once he got out the pen."

I gave her the lowdown on everything that was going on. Even told her about how his ex had confronted us at the Pub. I left out the part where Corey tried to call her the very next day. I needed his sister to be Team Tenosha. Not Team Dollie. *Fuck that bitch with a sick dick.*

"I can't stand Dollie. I wanted to whup her ass," Naomi confessed. "She'd never tell us whenever they would move Corey. And she was too hard to get in touch with. I remember so many times I wanted to go see my brother and never could because of her ass." She shook her head in revulsion. "My brother doesn't need somebody like that bitch."

I agreed with her. I decided to go ahead and tell her about the last time Dollie called Corey's phone. Well, I didn't tell her the whole story. Just the things my A1 Majesta said to her. We both rolled around on the bed, laughing hysterically until our sides hurt.

"If you ever beat her ass, call me! That's worth the trip to Abilene," Naomi said once she caught her breath.

We decided to go see if dinner was ready yet. Naomi also wanted to check on the kids. We headed down the stairs. We looked out the back door to make sure the kids were playing nicely. Then we helped Ms. Brenda finish making dinner in the kitchen.

Soon the food was ready. We got the children, cleaned them up, and sat them at the table to get their grub on. Once everybody had eaten the delicious meal, Ms. Brenda helped me get the kids settled in bed.

Naomi and Nestle said their good-byes soon after that. We sat in the living room, talking, until his mom retired up to her room. She was exhausted from everything. I was beginning to feel like I needed to lie down too. Corey turned and faced me.

"You really down for a nigga, ain't you?"

I looked up at him and nodded my head. I cuddled up beside him on the couch. He put his arm around me.

"You're the type of girl I'd want to spend the rest of my life with." He gently lifted up my chin and said to me, "Will you marry me?"

My heart skipped a thousand beats. I couldn't even begin to put into words the excitement that overcame me. The joy. The happiness. The one thing I wanted my children's father to see in me, Corey was able to. This man loved me and showed me every chance he could get. Now he was asking for my hand in marriage. I sat straight up and said yes to him. He kissed me softly.

"I can't wait for you to be my wife. You're so perfect for me."

We spent the rest of that weekend at his mom's house. We relaxed some. We even went to Fort Worth to do a little shopping for clothes and shoes. We took his mom out for lunch. Afterward, Corey left to meet up with Tiger and his family for a little bit. I remained behind with his mom and sister.

Quickly enough, our time to return home arrived. Once we were on the road, headed back to Abilene, a call came on my cell phone. It was Bruce. I answered.

"Say, where y'all at?" he asked me.

The way he sounded kind of scared me. I'd never heard my bro talk with such urgency.

"We're on our way back from Bedford. Why? What's up?" I said. Corey was driving, and I was in the passenger seat.

"Man, did you guys have any drugs or money at your house?" he asked.

I asked Corey, and he took the phone from me. They both talked for a while. I could tell by the way Corey was acting and by the way he sped up some that shit was not okay.

"Naw, I left the dope I had left and the pills with Drew," I heard Corey tell him. "Why? You out or something?"

"'Cause, man . . ."

I could hear what Bruce was saying to Corey as clear as day by the way he was yelling through the phone.

Bruce went on. "The landlord was there at the house, fixing the garage door for Ten. Task force ran through the house right when the landlord was getting ready to burn off. Ten has an eviction notice, and y'all got to be out by midnight tomorrow."

Chapter 29

Dollie

It had been a few weeks since I heard the truth about what Corey was really up to. I was beginning to get over that drama he had involved me in, and I had started mending my broken heart in the process. I started putting in some extra time at work and even began helping my uncle Justin at the bakery a couple of times a week. My new haircut was a brilliant idea. With the red highlights my beautician had given me to go along with the bob cut, not only was I beginning to feel like a new woman, but I even looked the part as well.

Everybody loved my new style. Plus, my aunt Audrina had hooked me up with the same Realtor who had helped her and my uncle find their house. We had started to meet a couple of times a week so we could explore houses that matched the criteria I had outlined. I still hadn't come across one that I really felt comfortable in. I hadn't discovered any that I immediately liked or felt safe in, either.

On top of that, my boss was offering to help put me through school so I could become a paralegal. While things could be better on the inside, everything appeared to be going well on the outside.

I had arrived at work thirty minutes early today. I needed to count the safe down and make the deposit at the bank for the week. I unlocked the door to let myself in. I made sure I locked it behind me, and then I headed to the back of the office. I had to give it to Jerry: he had a significant amount of space in his workplace. The whole headquarters had five separate rooms. Most of our clients had seen only Jerry's office and the front lobby, where my desk and Tammy's were located. A little hallway led to a cherrywood country-style kitchen with a fridge, stove, coffee machine, microwave, and minibar. That was where we normally ate our lunches.

Now, the kitchen was extremely large, but only a few people had ever been back there. They normally would come this way if they had to use the restroom or if a baby needed a diaper changed. The restroom was off to the side of the kitchen. When he first secured this office, Jerry had a girlfriend who was a painter, and she was dying to transform the space in his office. He allowed her to do over the restroom. She painted it light blue, with dark blue and white flowers along the base of the walls. The restroom was rather small, but it was comfortable. A large mirror had been placed above the sink, and there was enough counter space to lay a baby on. Luckily for me, all three of us were anal about keeping the restroom extremely clean and smelling good. We often took turns maintaining it at least three times a week, if not more.

If you looked in the kitchen, you'd see a door in the far left corner that had an exit sign over it. Any dummy would think that it led to the back alley of the building. But this was the door to the fifth room, which was located in the very back of the office. There used to be a back entrance, but Jerry had that sealed off. They had added a door at the far end of his too-large office, in case we needed to exit due to a fire. This room in the back was where Jerry kept all his files and stored condiments, toiletries, and the safe.

I was required to keep no more than 150 dollars in my desk drawer, and sometimes, if people paid on time, I had to count my drawer down twice a day. There were times when I didn't even have to worry about counting it down. because nobody made any payments. Jerry had stipulated that the safe could have only 475 dollars, and so I was required to count the safe down on Wednesdays and make a deposit at the bank for anything over that amount. Sometimes, I even found myself having to do it on Fridays.

I unlocked the back room and entered it, filled out the deposit slip, opened the safe, and dropped it down to the required amount. I locked the safe back up, making sure to twist the dial to "lose" the combination, exited the room, and locked the door tight behind me.

I headed back up front and placed my purse and truck keys inside my desk. I grabbed my office keys and let myself out, then bolted the door behind me. I had decided to walk down to the bank since it was right down the sidewalk. It was nice outside. Sometimes it was the little things, like nature and the birds chirping, that kept me sane. Made me appreciate life even more.

But right there on the sidewalk, I grew instantly paranoid. Something told me to check my surroundings. Right when I turned around to take in the scene, I caught sight of a red card sticking out from the window shield of my truck. I looked around me but didn't see a single soul in sight. I hurriedly grabbed the card and walked down the block to the bank. After I made the deposit, I finally took time out to read the message on the card.

Never let anybody tell you you're not worth it. You're a diamond in the rough, and if you were mine, I'd treat you like a queen. It was signed, *Secret admirer.*

My heart skipped a beat. *Is this for real?* I hurried up and walked back to the office and quickly unlocked the front door. I stepped inside and turned the CLOSED sign around so that it read OPEN. I immediately sat down and called my cousin Vic.

A grumpy voice filled the phone. "Hello?"

"Vic, you gotta wake up!" I was extremely excited and was unable to prevent that from showing.

A sense of adventure filled me. I mean, it wasn't every day that somebody left a card on your window. Some people would have been weirded out, but with the bullshit I had just gone through, I need to focus my attention on something else. Anything else, as long as it was worthy of my time.

"What the hell do you want, Doll? This shit better be good," Victoria whispered.

Ignoring her empty threat, I began to tell her about the card. I couldn't contain the joy that I was feeling. This card had my heart practically racing. By the time I was finished telling her about the card, I was damn near squealing like a pig.

Victoria sounded wide awake when she spoke again. "That haircut did you some good, after all. Any ideas?"

"No, but I hope he ain't ugly, and I hope he's my style," I said.

"Girl, I hope he ain't nothing like Corey's nothing ass." We both dissolved into a fit of giggles.

"I'm tired of feeling sad and empty."

"Good, Dollie. I'm going to pray that he is a real man and not half of one."

We chatted for a little bit before I hurried up and disconnected the phone call. The rest of the day went by smoothly. After work, I rushed across town to meet Rhonda, my Realtor, at this house she had told me was within my budget. The way she had made it sound, the house was to die for. I had called my aunt and given her the news about the house. Before I could even ask her to watch Drake, she offered to bring Drake home for me herself. My uncle Justin was going to meet me at the house Rhonda was showing me.

I turned onto the block the house was found on, and the first thing I noticed was lots of maple trees and honeysuckle bushes. You could tell the neighborhood was discreet and peaceful, and I was drawn to that right away. Altogether the houses on the avenue had an old Victorian look to them. The majority of the houses were well taken care of. They had either ivy vines growing up the sides and the front or maple trees towering gracefully around them. The branches seemed to hug the subdivision just right, adding a beautiful touch to it.

I immediately recognized my uncle's and Rhonda's cars parked in front of the house. I pulled into the driveway of my potential home. The house was white, with dark green shutters around the windows. The door was dark green. There was a white fence surrounding the property. The tips of the fence portion that separated my potential yard from the neighbors' were the same color as the door and shutters. The windows were fancy, and so was the screen door.

The front porch was huge, and it had a white railing going around it, except for where the stairs were. Ivy vines and white flowers covered the railing, making the house look so pretty and decorative.

Rhonda must have seen the look on my face. She walked over to me, with a huge grin spread across her face. She gave me a hug.

"This house is to die for, Dollie. It has your name written all over it."

My uncle walked around from the back and said the same exact thing that Rhonda had just said. The three of us walked up the porch steps together, and Rhonda opened the door.

As soon as we entered, I immediately fell in love. The living room was a nice size. It had cream-colored carpeting and whitewashed walls. There was a long hallway that stretched from the living room. Once I started to walk down the hall, I noticed the entrance to the kitchen. The kitchen had hardwood floors, and it had a cozy layout reminiscent of a cabin. It had a brand-new stove and refrigerator.

A back door led from the kitchen to a huge backyard, which was surrounded by a privacy fence in the same color as the fence around the front lawn but slightly taller. When you stepped out the back door, you ended up on a nice deck that was covered around the sides. It opened in the front, onto the backyard. The yard itself was huge, with plenty of room for my son to run around and play freely.

I returned to the hallway and toured a large bathroom. The bathroom had a black-tile floor and a big mirror. In front of the mirror was a long cabinet in which two sinks rested. The bathtub was big enough for three people. The toilet looked brand new. I exited the bathroom and continued walking to the end of the hall. There the master bedroom was on one side, and a smaller bedroom was on the other side. Both were nice-sized rooms and had cream-colored carpeting and walk-in closets. In the master bedroom, there was a bathroom that was identical to the first bathroom except for the fact that it also had a stand-alone shower in it. Boy, was I smitten.

"The owner of the house would like to rent it out for now. They are not sure if they want to sell it yet," Rhonda began. "Is that okay with you?"

"Hell yeah! I don't mind renting this house."

With that said, Rhonda and I started the paperwork. My uncle called my aunt to let her know I was taking the house. Before he got off the phone with her, he handed it to me.

"Auntie?" I said.

"Dollie," I heard her say. "Remember when I asked you if you believed you were worth more than what you were settling for?"

"Yes, ma'am."

"How do you feel now?"

"I feel like I'm worth a million bucks and then some!" I shouted, unable to contain my happiness.

"That's my Doll!" She laughed.

Chapter 30

Rhonda delivered my house key to me four days after I filled out the paperwork. That was when I was going to have the deposit and the first month's rent for her. My aunt and uncle were so happy I had found a house, they gave me money to pay an extra month's rent as a gift. I had to admit I was on cloud nine. They say when you take out the trash, your blessings start coming down. I was a true testimony of that.

I had agreed to open up my uncle's bakery since Victoria could not get there until noon. It was a Saturday, so I didn't mind. Rhonda had agreed to meet me there, since I would be the only one at the shop. After she arrived, I signed the lease agreement, paid her, and proudly put my new key on my key ring. My uncle had baked Rhonda a seven-layer chocolate cake. I helped her get it into her car. This was an appreciation cake. I needed this new start. I wanted this badly, to the point where I was craving a new chapter in my life.

Business was slow. After Rhonda left, the morning kind of dragged by, until about eleven thirty, when some of the local neighborhood kids poured into the shop to get either some fudge or sugar cookies. A couple of moms came into the store to place birthday cake orders. Victoria arrived right after they left.

"Hey, *chica pequeña!*" my cousin sang out as she tied her apron around her, then clocked in.

"Hey, big cousin," I said happily.

She congratulated me on my new home. I showed her the pictures I had taken with my cell phone. We oohed and aahed over them together. Right when we both finished scrolling through the pictures, customers started walking in. Soon after their orders had been filled and they had left, even more people started to pour into the bakery. My shift was technically over, but I stayed to help Victoria out. She checked the customers out after I gave them the goodies they wanted.

Forty-five minutes after the rush began, the crowd died down. Victoria talked me into staying a little bit longer while she ran to the back to pop some cinnamon rolls and cookies into the oven. She also wanted to whip up a German chocolate cake since we were down to the last one. I got to work cleaning the countertop, and then I rearranged the display, as we had sold out of certain cookies and cakes. Right when I was done removing the last tray, Bruce and Drew walked in.

I hadn't seen Drew since I slammed the door in his face. As for Bruce, I wasn't expecting to run into him, period. I was very upset with him and felt like I hated him. I felt like he was the main culprit who had helped Corey and that fat bitch get together. He'd smiled to my face and laughed at me behind my back. I despised his bitch ass. I demanded to be respected. Therefore, a huge part of me wanted to curse his lame ass out and demand an apology in the process. I was better than that, though. Just as quickly as my face got hot, I plastered a fake grin on it by thinking about my new house. That helped change my attitude from Little Miss Attitude galore to pure joy. I took a deep breath and greeted them.

"Can I get you anything?" I asked.

They both shook their heads as they walked around, looking at the newly arranged display. Bruce got on his phone, probably to call his wife and get clarification about a cake, or at least that was the way it sounded to me. While he talked, Drew walked over to me.

"I like your haircut," he said, admiring my new do.

"Thanks, Drew," I replied cheerfully.

He looked a little taken aback by my enthusiasm, which made me want to laugh. I guessed by our last encounter, he was expecting the worst outcome possible. I had to admit, he was courageous to hold a conversation with me now, after the way I had blown up at him.

"Sorry about the other night," he began to explain. "I didn't mean to upset you in any way."

I put my head down in shame. I began to walk over to the cash register. I looked back over at him. "You are okay, Drew. I shouldn't have directed my anger toward you. I'm sorry too."

He walked over and shook my hand. We both started laughing. We began to hold a decent conversation. I was surprised how easy it was to have a conversation with him.

"You know I got a new house, right?" I quizzed him.

"Nope. I didn't hear that. Where is it at?" he asked, curious.

I told him where it was located, with the stipulation that he kept it to himself. He agreed.

"Maybe I'll come by and see for myself. Just don't slam the door in my face," he joked.

"My bad, I said!" I laughed at him.

Bruce motioned to let Drew know that he was ready. He wanted the double-layer carrot cake and some brownies. I immediately got to work putting his order in our specialty boxes and then topping them both off with a ribbon. I rang up the order, Bruce paid for it, and then we all said good-bye. Just then, Victoria emerged from the back.

"I got it from here, Doll," she said. "I can get some baking done until the next little rush."

"You sure, cousin?" I asked, unsure about that.

Both of us looked at the display. I helped her stock it back up with more cookies, cakes, and brownies. She had three red velvet cakes baking. I could see that two sheets of raisin cookies, chocolate chips, and sugar cookies had been set off to the side to cool.

"This will be enough to help me get through the next rush. Plus, two more employees will be here shortly. I can handle it from here, cuzzo."

"Okay, cousin," I said to her.

I happily clocked out. I removed my apron and went to the back to hang it up. I gave Victoria her keys, which I'd used to open the store. We both hugged. She congratulated me on my new home once again. I reminded her to call me if she needed any more help. I walked out and looked up at the sky. It was time for my son and I to get settled into our new house.

Chapter 31

That weekend, I spent a lot of it buying new furniture to complement our home. I loaded up my truck with our clothes, my son's toys, my movies, and everything else and moved all of it into our new house. The utilities were already turned on. Rhonda had allowed me to do that before I even signed the lease, under the condition that I didn't tell anybody she let me do it. I had also arranged for the movers to deliver my furniture between 3:00 and 5:00 p.m. on Monday. My uncle had assured me that either he or Victoria would be there to let them in.

Jazzy, my best friend, was here for the weekend. She helped me pick out rugs and mirrors to hang up in the house. We had just laid down the last sheepskin in my little boy's room when Jazzy turned around to face me. She rested her tiny frame against the wall. One of her long curls had escaped her ponytail, and it rested gently against her cheek.

"So, what's next?" she asked.

I looked around. Half of me was in a daze. The other half was proud of me. I felt like pinching myself to make sure I was not dreaming. I opted to sit on my son's floor instead. Feeling the carpet was surreal enough to me. I was cheesing from the inside out. I rested my chin on my knees. I thought about my friend's question and shrugged my shoulders as a response.

Good really could come out of something bad. Even after you gave your heart and soul to somebody who clearly didn't want them—who didn't cherish you or even know your worth—you could still stand tall, with your head held high, and make shit happen for yourself.

A few things still bothered me about this whole ordeal. I'd be lying if I pretended that they did not. Like how did everybody see what was going on except me? All that time I had wasted on a man who obviously didn't care, who played me like the strings on a guitar. Somebody who left me for somebody who was less than a woman. A broken-down mutt with four kids. Now what the hell was that fool going to do with that?

And what kind of woman would ride around in somebody else's car? What kind of woman would think it was cute to treat somebody else like that? I would hate for her to go through some bullshit behind him. It would come to her. I said this to myself all the time. *The way it begins is the way it will end.* I didn't know if it made me feel better, but the more I told myself this, the more it helped me to be able to face tomorrow.

I did have to admit that it had ruined my heart, like a glass that disintegrated into a mountain of pieces when you threw it against a wall. But the pain that came after it hurt even worse. It didn't make that much sense for someone to ache like that. Time did mend all wounds. I did have to acknowledge that my spirits weren't suffering anywhere near as much as they were at first. If anything, this whole ordeal had given me strength and shown me what I was really worth. Like my uncle Justin always said, "When one door closes, God always opens another."

"You miss him, don't you?" Jazzy's piercing question interrupted my thoughts.

I looked at her, startled, and when I realized who "him" was, I shook my head. After you endured that kind of pain, how could you? What woman in her right mind would want to return to somebody who publicly humiliated her the way he had me? That wasn't love. Only a no-good snake with no heart would play a sick game like that. I had no respect left for him at all.

"I was just thinking about how love is a game. Anybody can play, and the players involved can either make or break your heart, if you let them."

Jazzy looked off into space and then slowly sank to a sitting position on the floor. She sat Indian-style, resting her back against the wall. She began chewing on her lower lip, contemplating what to say next.

"At least you know what it's like to be in love. People look high and low for it and never can find it."

I raised my head up and met Jazzy's eyes. "The pain I was feeling was no joke. It's fucked up that some ignorant-ass fool can play with your heart like that." I sighed and looked away. "To me, Jazzy, that's not love. Love is not a one-way street at all."

Jazzy smiled. "Look at you now, though. You're doing so much better. You look healthier. Your hair . . . oh, my God . . . you cut it all off! But you are still one beautiful person. You got a house, Doll. Everything you want, you have."

"Except for Corey," I replied sadly as a feeling of hurt passed over me again.

"Except a *man*, not Corey," Jazzy said, correcting me. She sprang up from the floor, then rubbed her flat stomach. "Corey's not a man. He's a little boy doing little boy things. He will never realize what he has until it's gone. Anyway, girlfriend, don't you see what you can accomplish once you rid yourself of trash?"

"Yes, ma'am!" I smiled happily to myself.

"Now, let's go get our grub on, girl. I'm starving."

Chapter 32

By the end of the week, my little boy and I were fully established in our new home. Drake loved the fact he had his own bedroom. My little man was ready to do big boy things, like dress himself and brush his little bitty teeth.

I was happy to have my own space, my own kitchen, and a backyard. Pretty much my own everything, period. Jazzy had already left Abilene. Before she'd left, she held a surprise housewarming party for me, alongside my cousin Vic. All my other friends had come to the party to see my new place and celebrate with me.

When I returned home that Friday, with Drake in tow, I immediately began to prepare dinner. I was making us steak fajitas. Drake settled into his new room and began playing with his building blocks while I cooked. I could hear the movie *The Smurfs* playing in his room.

After we ate dinner, I cleaned up the kitchen and got Drake ready for bed. Then I hopped in the shower and washed my hair. When I was done, I slipped on a pair of red-and-white Adidas wind pants and a white beater. Then I tucked Drake in bed, grabbed the latest *People* magazine, and curled up on the couch to look through it.

I was halfway done reading the piece they had done on Muhammad Ali when I heard a loud knock on my front door. I jumped at first, wondering who would be knocking at this time of night. After making sure to mark the page I was on, I quickly placed my mag down. I got up and turned the porch light on first. I peeked through the window and saw no one on the porch. I opened the door and found a card with a single rose taped to the other side of the door. I stepped outside and looked around. No sign of humanity anywhere.

I gently pulled the card and the rose off the door and walked over to the swinging chair my uncle Justin had set up for me on my front porch. I opened the card. I read it aloud to myself.

"I can't hide my feelings for you any longer. Please, meet me here at seven o' clock tomorrow evening. Love, your secret admirer."

"Whoa!" I said aloud to myself.

He wanted to reveal himself to me. My mind raced as I tried to figure out who it could be. Unfortunately, my mind was blank.

I tried to finish reading the article in the magazine when I returned inside, but my mind was fixated on what I had just received. I tried to go to sleep. That proved to be futile, because I was restless. I stirred in my sleep constantly. Turning in my bed all throughout the night due to my mind racing meant that I did not get adequate rest.

I didn't know what time it was when I finally fell asleep, but I was woken up around eight. Drake was hungry and was making it his business to let me know that. Feeling groggy, I got up to feed my growing boy. After all, a mother had to do what she was supposed to do. I headed down the hall, toward the kitchen. I looked at the counter on which I had placed the card and the rose, and I felt a renewed energy.

I made homemade biscuits, sausage, and scrambled eggs with cheese for my son. After he was done eating, I got him dressed for the day. I watched him brush his teeth and wash his face. He went out the back door to play in the sandbox. I went outside to make sure all the gates were locked. I left the back door open and sat in a kitchen chair and observed him through the opening in the deck. I reached for my cell and called Jazzy.

A sleepy Jazzy answered the phone. As I filled her in on what was going on, she became wide awake.

"Bitch, who you think it is?" she asked

I smiled at myself. "Girl, I don't know who it is, but whoever it is, I hope he ain't no Michael Myers son of a bitch."

She burst out laughing. "I am so happy for you, girl. God had a plan for you, and maybe you had to go through all that to get here."

I silently agreed. A strange feeling seemed to cleanse my wounded heart.

As I sat there finishing up my conversation with Jazzy, a huge part of me wanted 7:00 p.m. to hurry up and get here. I hung up the phone and went outside to join my little boy. We stayed outside for most of the morning. We ate lunch on the deck, and Drake took a nap right after we finished. While he was sleeping, his grandma called. She wanted him to come stay the night with her. I got his overnight bag ready, making sure to pack his Sunday school clothes too.

When he finally woke up, I gave him a good bath to wash the sand off of him. I dressed him in a nice polo shirt, a pair of brown corduroy pants, and a pair of his white-and-blue Polo shoes. I loaded him in the truck and took him to his grandma's. I stayed and chatted with her for a while. Afterward, I stopped at the bakery on my way home. My uncle Justin had taken the day off, but my aunt Audrina was working, while Victoria and the new baker my uncle had hired were in the back, baking birthday cakes and making more fudge. I stayed and talked with my aunt for a while, filling her in on what was going on.

When I got back to the house, I realized it was five o'
clock. I popped in my Beyoncé CD and cranked that ho up
while I cleaned the living room and the front bathroom.
I started a load of Drake's clothes. Then, I began to get
ready to meet my mystery man. I hopped in the shower.
I dried off and lotioned up really good when I was done.
I put a dab of J.Lo's Glow perfume behind my knees, on
my wrists, and behind my ears. I put on my True Religion
blue jean skirt and a red cropped T-shirt that barely
covered my midriff but accentuated my sexy shape. I slid
on a pair of my red Chanel sandals and, of course, topped
my outfit off with my signature gold hoop earrings. I then
curled my bob, making sure it was layered in the back to
show off my cut. I was pleased with my hairstyle choice,
and I knew I was looking like a bad bitch today!

Once I was done, it was about 6:45 p.m. I walked into
the living room and turned off my CD. I put Drake's
clothes in the dryer and then started a load of my own
clothes.

I decided to go outside to wait for my admirer. As I
walked out, to my surprise, I saw Drew standing there
with a single rose. Before I could say anything at all, he
wrapped his arms around my waist and kissed me.

Chapter 33

Tenosha

My world was in turmoil. Once we finally arrived back at the crib, I was finally able to assess the scene before me. I wasn't prepared. My kids were not, either. My house was completely trashed. The law had totally ransacked my house. It was so bad, I had no idea where to go, what to do, who to call, or anything. I was just standing there like a statue, as if I had been cemented permanently to the spot in which I was standing. I wanted to cry, but no tears fell down. Was I shocked? That was an understatement.

Corey was on his phone, hitting people up. Right then my little brother and sister appeared at my home. Drew was carrying trash bags filled with his things. He looked over at me.

"I left her, sis," Drew said.

I couldn't even talk. I was at a loss for words. My kids were starting to fuss because they were sleepy. It appeared as if the oldest ones had no problem tramping over the heap of garbage spread out before us. Karen, my one-year-old, sat on the floor and fussed. The only fucking thing was their bedrooms weren't their bedrooms anymore. Every inch of every single part of every room in my house was totally fucked up.

Dressers had been turned over; mattresses had been flipped and cut up. My fucking clothes were all over the place. I had socks and underwear in the goddamned bathroom, where they didn't even belong. My entire household had been demolished. I walked like a zombie, looking at each horrid scene before me. I picked Karen up, and when I finally made it back to what we used to call the damn living room, I sat down on my upside-down coffee table. I looked helplessly at Justine.

"What do I do, Justine?" I whispered.

We locked eyes with each other. Neither one of us moved. Her eyes were filled with a mixture of pity and confusion. I was willing to bet she felt just as helpless as I did the moment my foot hit the front door. I wanted her to wave a magic wand around and make this shit just, *poof*, go away. This was the real world. Fast living didn't quite operate like that.

"Sis, I wish I knew. I'm trying to think it out too."

"Justine—" I began to protest, but just then Marie, my oldest daughter, wandered over to me.

"Mama, I'm sleepy?" Poor thing was so tired, her statement came out more like a question.

She climbed into my lap, next to Karen, and tried to get comfortable so she could get some rest. My other two children crowded around me. They were ready for bed too. Even though they didn't come right out and say it, I knew they just were not sure where they could lay their heads. It literally broke my fuckin' heart.

"Let me call Grandma and see if the kids can stay with her for a while," Justine said, then walked outside, dialing our grandma's number at the same time.

"What the fuck am I supposed to do?" I shrieked. Tears started falling down my face. I didn't bother to wipe them off. I just let them fall freely down my face. My oldest son leaned over, trying his best to keep my face tear free with his little hands. That act right there made a bitch cry beyond intense. I was feeling less than a woman right now. My children couldn't even sleep in their own beds right now.

Corey came over and stroked my face a little. He instructed the three older children to sit down at the kitchen table. He was trying to straighten things up the best way he could. At least the kitchen table was standing and chairs surrounded it. They could at least sit down. My baby girl remained in my lap, fast asleep.

He smoothed away my tears, assuring me everything would be okay. I looked up at him. I wondered if them muthafuckas had even found any dope here.

"Did we have drugs here? I mean, what was going on?"

"I don't know, babe."

"How in the hell am I supposed to move, baby?" I asked. "I have to be at work at nine in the morning."

"How are *we* supposed to move?" he joked, cracking a smile.

I didn't find this situation exactly humorous, considering my babies were exhausted and their beds were all fucked up. He hurriedly recanted his comment once he understood I didn't consider this a laughing matter.

"We got this, man. Don't worry," he said. "They didn't find shit. Plus, we have the money, and Drew has the drugs." Corey looked at my brother, and he nodded his head. "I'll call Kitty and get her to rent us a room at Motel Six."

"Yeah, sis. I didn't even bring it with me over here. I left it in a safe place over at Justine's place," Drew stated. That made me feel a little bit better.

Just then, Justine walked in. "Grandma said she'll keep the kids. Mom said she'll help too."

"Did you tell her what was going on?" I asked.

"Hell naw. You know damn well Grandma and Mom would flip the fuck out," my sister said.

"Yeah, they would have told your ass to deal with it," Drew added.

The three of us agreed not to say anything to my grandma and them about what was going on right now. Not until I was able to talk to them myself, one-on-one. Drew and Corey drilled it into the kids sleepy heads what they could and could not say while they were over there.

Justine searched around the kitchen floor until she located some trash bags. Drew and Hanson went to help her load the kids' clothes into them. Marie and Tyrese filled other trash bags with their belongings, things they couldn't see themselves going without.

"Don't overdo it, you guys! I don't need Grandma to contemplate that you guys are moving in. It's only temporary," I instructed, raising my voice so they could hear me.

A chorus of voices yelled back, "Okay."

I couldn't move from my spot on the coffee table. My body was frozen. The task force had come in and ruined my home. *For what*? I asked myself. Did that mean we were hot now? I was sure we had not been calling attention to ourselves. Did somebody tell on us? What the fuck was going on? So many questions and different scenarios were running over and over in my mind. This whole situation had me feeling a bit uneasy and pretty pissed off now. I felt like a switch had turned off the sadness and self-pity but had converted it to anger.

I was still seated on my coffee table when Justine and Drew loaded up the Expedition. Did I kiss my kids good-bye? Because I didn't remember. I just didn't know what I was going to do next. My mind was racing a mile a minute. I thought for an instant to call my baby daddy. I longed to do so, honestly. I knew that if I was with his ass still, I would still have a fuckin' home and wouldn't have the law targeting my ass. For the first time, I admitted to myself that the grass might not be so green on the other side of the fence, after all.

While Justine and Drew were gone, Bruce arrived with Majesta. My best friend came over and hugged me. That was when I let loose. I couldn't control the tears escaping my eyes.

"Don't worry, Ten," she said, gently wrapping her long arms around me in a protective way. "We'll get you moved out," she promised.

"It's not even that, Majesta. Did you see my kids? Everything was just fine when we left. We come back to the fuckin' crib, and the fuckin' pigs literally destroyed my damn home!"

"I know they had the whole damn block sewed up, sis, for real." Majesta gave a play-by-play on what she had observed going on. "That's when Bruce hit your line," she added.

My head was spinning. They had come into my place, hoping to find something. I was glad they couldn't find shit. But I was pissed off that my furniture had been destroyed in their effort to catch us with some shit. I was going to have to start all over and obtain everything again. It had taken me and my baby daddy years to get our home looking the way it had, and just like that the Abilene Police Department had come and fucked it all up.

"My job, though. I have to go to work tomorrow. I can't stay up all night!" I said.

"You won't miss work, and you won't have to worry about anything. I got you, baby girl," Corey said. "You heard me on the phone with the dope fiend. We getting a room right now, so don't even trip. You'll be able to rest your pretty little head soon, Tenosha. Everything is going to be all right," he added, trying to reassure me.

"Okay, Corey, I trust you," I said. Truth was, I wasn't quite sure how I was feeling right now. Too many unanswered questions and missing puzzle pieces.

We waited for Justine and Drew to get back and passed the time pretty much in silence. Occasionally, Majesta and Corey made small talk. I opted not to jump in it. I had more important shit running through my mind at that moment. When my little brother and my sister finally returned, Corey left in the rental to get one of the dope fiends to rent our room for us.

"Did Grandma say anything?" I asked.

Justine and Drew both shook their heads.

"The kids were knocked out by the time we got there," my sister said.

"Yeah, we helped Grandma get them in the bed," Drew said, chiming in.

When Corey returned, he came back with two keys, one for us and the other for Drew. The boys stayed up front talking, while my sister, Majesta, and I went in the bedroom and put my and Corey's clothes into trash bags. Drew, Corey, and Majesta then loaded the clothes up in the Expedition. Justine and I sat in the middle of the torn-up bedroom.

"Justine, don't say a word." I dropped my voice down to a whisper. She leaned in closer to listen. "I feel like if I had just stayed with Bobbie, I wouldn't be going through this."

"That's crazy, Tenosha, because Drew was saying that. He's really upset, even though it's not showing right now. He ain't feeling this shit," Justine murmured back.

"Man, he did try to warn me, though, sis. Not going to lie."

"You going to leave Corey or what?"

I paused for a second before I began. I gave her the rundown on what had happened in Bedford. Her eyes lit up in surprise when I mentioned to her about him proposing to me.

"I'm in too deep now. I have to ride this shit out. I won't give Bobbie the satisfaction of trying to go back to him. I just won't," I said.

Right then we heard footsteps coming down the hall and immediately knew we were going to have to switch up the subject. Justine eyes widened as she looked around the room. I clutched her hand. We burst out laughing before we turned our attention back to what was going on around us.

"Whoever did this seems mad," Justine said.

I looked up at her. "Whoever did what?"

"The law, girl. They didn't just search your house. They tore this whole damn place up!" Justine said. She rose to her feet. She stood over me, then presented her hands. I caught them with mine and held on tightly. She pulled me up off the floor.

"They know what's going on, Tenosha. They were pissed because they couldn't find shit. I don't think you should *not* be worried. Just be careful."

"They're watching us," I said.

We looked at each other for a brief moment. An eerie feeling crept through me. We needed to hurry up and get the hell out of here. I started for the door, but my sister grabbed my arm,

"Yeah, sis, and I think somebody is telling on y'all too."

My thoughts exactly.

Chapter 34

My night in that room Corey rented, which was at Motel 6, wasn't too great. I needed sleep, but I just ended up tossing and turning until it was time for me to get up and get ready for work. Just like Corey had promised, they moved all my things out of my house and put them in storage while I was at work the next day. Corey had me take the Expedition to work. Bruce arrived with a U-Haul truck he got for us when it was time for Corey and Drew to move my shit out.

We stayed at Motel 6 for almost a week and a half. The smoker who was letting us use the Expedition let us keep it for another week. Corey was trying to lay low, but the weekend after the eviction, he met the connect in Eastland again. He was determined to make something shake so we could get into a new spot. He returned with more dope and pills.

I was getting the hang of my new job and was beginning to pull a full forty hours a week. I'd been hired part-time, but my current situation called for desperate measures. I had had no choice but to take those hours once I learned they were available.

Plus, I was hitting the block with my soon-to-be husband. When I wasn't with him, I'd check on my kids. I never stayed long. My grandma was pissed off. Somehow word got back to her about what had really happened. She cussed my ass out black and blue when I stopped by one day to drop food off for the kids.

She even hurled her *chanclas* at me. They missed my nose by an inch. I was almost afraid she wasn't going to keep my children anymore. She hurled insults at me, told me I was a bad mom for choosing a man over my kids. Told me I should have stayed with Bobbie. He wouldn't have put me in a position where I didn't have a place to lay my head. She had never really liked Corey. Now that she knew what was going on, she loathed him. She felt like this condition we were all in was absolutely his fault.

In the midst of being homeless, Corey was hell-bent on throwing an engagement party. We planned to rent the ballroom at the Royal Inn. After that, he wanted to try to find an apartment.

One day I returned to the motel room after work to find it empty. Bruce, Justine, and Corey were in the neighborhood. They said money was rolling. I jumped in the shower, and after I got out, made me some noodles. Once I was finishing eating up my food, my brother hit my line.

"Hey, Drew," I answered as I settled into my bed.

"Hey, Ten," he replied.

Drew was calling to let me know about an apartment that was up for rent. The apartment was at the top of a garage behind somebody's house. He had overheard Grandma telling Mom about it when he stopped by to check on the kids for me. He'd played it off like he wasn't listening. He confided that she was going to tell our uncle about it, so he could move out of her house. Not if I could get to it first, though.

"Come get me," I said.

Straightaway, I phoned Corey and let him in on what I was currently getting prepared to check out. I put on a pair of jeans, a white T-shirt, and some white Nikes. I combed my hair and put it in a ponytail. Drew pulled up twenty minutes later. I grabbed my key and hopped into the green Cadillac he was driving.

"All they want is three hundred a month, with a hundred-dollar deposit," Drew explained as he drove out of the parking lot.

"Did you go by there first?" I quizzed him.

"Nah. I just heard Grandma telling Mom about it. I knew I had to let you know about it first."

"Damn. Is she that mad at me that she wouldn't tell me first? I have kids!"

Drew just shook his head and shrugged his shoulders. I understood she was mad at me, but I already felt bad enough that I had lost my kids' childhood home. I was avoiding being around Grandma and Mom as much as possible. You would think they would want me to hurry up and obtain housing so I could get my daughters and sons back.

Lately, even Bobbie had been blowing up my line. I didn't even feel like arguing with my kids' pops. As far as I was concerned, I was trying my hardest to get my shit together. I didn't need his ass rubbing my recent failures in my face, either. My family had already made me feel like I was a horrible mom, and I didn't need the father of my children telling me this at the same damn time.

We pulled up to the house twenty minutes later. It was located on the Southside, close to a neighborhood where a bunch of Mexicans lived. It sat directly in front of a school where they used to send bad children. They called it RAC. Today a lot of children were playing football in the open field that was across the street. I didn't care, as long as I could have a residence of my own to stay in. Not no damn hotel room. A home.

Drew called the lady, and she came out of the house five minutes later. She was a fat Mexican lady with a heavy accent. She wore glasses and appeared to be extremely friendly. She greeted us and shook both of our hands. She motioned for us to follow her.

She led us to the back of the property and then up some sturdy stairs next to the garage. As we walked up, she talked about how all the bills were included in the rent. They didn't mind parties, but not on weeknights. All she asked was that we give them a heads-up if we were to have a social gathering. That seemed reasonable enough for me. She told us that it was just her and her husband. That they were both retired and owned several homes, though they were all out of this area.

After we walked up the stairs behind her, she opened the door to the apartment. It had one big room in front, which was the living room. It didn't have central heat and air. Only AC units were in the rooms, and a water heater was against the back wall of the living room. The kitchen was rather small, only big enough for two people at a time.

The bathroom was small as well, and when you turned the water on, the pipes made loud clattering thuds. As I was expecting, the two bedrooms were small. The walls in each room were a dingy brown color. The carpet was an extremely ugly gray color. All I could do was stare. I was not quite sure why they thought it was okay to have the interior of the home decorated in those weird colors like that.

The windows were rather small in the living room and bedrooms. You could tell nobody had cleaned them in a while, as they looked very dusty. They had, at least, put a brand-new stove and refrigerator in the small kitchen. The new whiteness stood out in contrast to the ugly wall color and the yellow tiled floor. The whole place was small and needed lots of help, but you know what? It was better than a hotel. And something my pockets definitely could afford.

"I'll take it," I told the lady.

She went downstairs to get the papers for me to fill out. I called Corey and asked him to get over here with the money.

"How much is it?" he asked.

I told him the price.

"Is it nice?"

"It's decent enough for us to live in without wasting money on a fuckin' hotel room every day."

He said he was on his way. By the time the lady returned and I had filled the papers out, my man showed up with the money. He gave her the deposit and the first month's rent. With that, she handed me the keys to my new place.

I decided to let my kids stay with my grandma until after our engagement party. Now that we had our own spot, I felt we had even more of a reason to celebrate. Not only our engagement, but being able to bounce back after a hater tried to fuck us with the law.

In the end Corey decided to go on ahead and rent that ballroom at the Royal Inn for the party. I filled out invitations for everybody we knew. I made sure to invite Tiger and Naomi. Corey and I also changed our rental cars up. We no longer had the Expedition, so we rented a white Avalanche from Enterprise. Actually, the same guy who owned the Expedition agreed to rent this car for us for a couple of weeks. This guy also went on ahead and traded some dope for a vehicle, a red Kia, from one of our clients for the week. Corey kept the Avalanche, and I drove the red Kia.

It was going to be a crazy week, and two cars were a must. My brother, Drew, had moved in with us, since he'd decided to leave Koa's crazy ass. He was always dipping in and out, so I never knew when he was going to be home. He was close to Bruce, anyhow, and therefore, he often ended up spending a lot of his time at Bruce and Justine's place.

My new landlord didn't mind that we were always coming and going. Corey was pushing that white girl extra hard just so we wouldn't break ourselves. Corey claimed he knew how to throw a party. He told me he'd take care of everything. I hadn't seen much of him since the day he paid for the ballroom. He would be gone all day, but he always made sure he was in the house and in bed by midnight. I loved the way he made me feel. He was different from my baby daddy. For a moment, I was worried I had made a bad decision, but now I realized I had not at all.

All Bobbie did was work. Nothing was good enough for him. I was decent enough only to make our little sweethearts for him. That was it. He had never told me he loved me. Bobbie had always played around and had taken his verbal abuse too far at times. Corey was so different. He was the best thing that had ever happened to me. He treated me like a queen, and I deserved that. I deserved him. I was worthy of every little thing he had to offer.

The night before the party, Corey arrived home shortly after I got off of work. He was sitting on the couch when I came out of the bathroom. I had just gotten out of the shower and was surprised to see him home so early.

"Ran out of dope," he said before I could ask anything. He was flipping aimlessly through the channels on the TV.

I dried my hair off with a towel and let my thick curls fall loosely around my neck. I checked around the house to see if Drew was home. No sign of my brother anywhere. I walked into the kitchen and cooked us both a hamburger real quick.

When I was done, I gave Corey a plate with a burger resting on it, accompanied by a tall glass of iced sweet tea.

Without any questions, he took the plate and ate. When he was finished, I took his plate back and put it in the sink. I stood in the kitchen and wolfed the rest of my food down. I washed both plates off. Afterward, I sat down next to him. Corey had a small box sitting on his lap.

I gazed up at him. "What's that, babe?" I pointed at the box.

He opened it, and without a word, he slipped a single diamond ring on my finger. "I'm going to marry you on Monday."

I looked down at my ring and back up at him. I felt like a giddy little schoolgirl who had just learned her crush liked her too. I kissed my soon-to-be husband.

"Why so soon?" I asked softly.

"'Cause you're a good gal. You don't deserve to be kept from your kids right now. Somebody hated on us. I feel bad because you having to go through this bullshit. At the same time, though, I wouldn't want to go through this with anybody else but you."

"Thank you," I whispered. "I love you and only you. I love you so much, Corey!"

He kissed me, and when he finally released me, he said to me, "A lot of people might be mad because I'm with you. Fuck them. You are all I want."

That brought great comfort to my heart. A huge part of me felt like marrying on Monday meant moving rather fast. Not only that, but I was dreaming of a huge wedding. His date for our marriage did not give me enough time to pull a large affair together. As if he had read my mind, he gave me the answer I needed.

"We will have a real wedding later. Bonnie and Clyde style."

The next day, Friday, dawned, and I could barely contain my excitement. My engagement party was that night.

My boss had allowed me to have that day and Saturday off. Majesta, Justine, and I were going to take the Chevy Avalanche to Dallas to get our outfits. Corey was going to keep the Kia.

We headed to South Dallas to get our outfits from JT's. The trip didn't take as long as we had expected it would. When we got back to Abilene, I made it a point to stop by and see my kids at my grandma's. Of course, she was on one. She was mad I hadn't come by since Tuesday to see them. I assured her I'd be there tomorrow evening to take them home.

When we arrived at my house, Drew, Bruce, Corey, Meaty, and Kid were there, getting ready. Meaty was the big homie from the neighborhood. He had just got out of prison two days ago. His face resembled a pit bull's, and he was tall and huge. He was a big ole teddy bear, but when it was time to fight, that nigga was in the middle of everything. He loved fighting and loved knocking people out.

Kid was Meaty's protégé. Whatever Meaty did, Kid was right there. I knew for sure that when Meaty did his three-year sentence, Kid kept it one hundred and looked after Meaty's two daughters and kept money on his books. Kid was a dope boy, but he took the big homie's advice and went legit. He got himself a job at Walmart and worked there the entire time Meaty was locked up. They both wanted to come and give me their blessings before the party.

Drew was making everybody a shot, and Bruce was rolling up two sweets when we walked in.

"Y'all, don't get too fucked up before the party," I joked.

Majesta, Justine, and I gathered in my bedroom to get ready. Justine hopped in the shower first. While she was taking her shower, Majesta flatironed my hair for me.

When Justine came out, I hopped in the shower, making sure not to get my hair wet. When I was done, Majesta went in. I had gotten a badass True Religion outfit to go with the yellow pumps I had bought a while ago. My outfit was going to go well with Corey's Gucci outfit, the one he had been talking about wearing for our party. When I came out of the bedroom, I heard a whistle from Kid.

"Look at my baby," Corey said as he took my hand and spun me around.

We all chilled around the house, smoking and drinking until it was time for us to leave for the Royal Inn. While we were on the road, Naomi called to let us know she was thirty minutes away. She was bringing her new boyfriend along for us to meet.

That night was a blur to me. The ballroom was spectacular. Corey never left my side, and we were both fucked up. All of his homies showed up. My friends and family showed up as well. One of my cousins had gotten us an engagement cake. That was all gone within a matter of minutes. Then everybody crowded around to see my new ring. Corey was proud to show off his soon-to-be wife. That night was incredible.

Toward the end of the night, right when we were slowly getting ready to split, Corey got a call on his phone. I knew it was about money, because I saw Young Soljah hand over some issue to Corey.

"Say, baby, you gonna have to drive," Corey said to me. "I'm lit up. Plus, we gotta hit this lick real quick. They talkin' money, baby."

"Where to?" I asked as we headed outside.

I hopped into the driver's side of the car. He got in the passenger's side. I was messed up, but I felt like I could still operate a car.

"They gonna meet us at the cleaners on Dansville."

I headed in that direction. Corey was separating the dope up and turned up the volume on the stereo. The speakers were blaring out slam jams. I started singing to Alicia Key's "Doesn't Mean Anything."

When I finally got there, Corey motioned for me to get out of the car. We both got out and walked over to a Dodge Challenger. The client was waiting on us. A person I didn't recognize was sitting on the passenger side, but I didn't care too much. I was faded. Corey had me take the money from the dope fiend. I took the money and stumbled back to our car. Corey gave him the dope and followed close behind me. After we got into our car, I started to drive off. Not even halfway down the street, I heard sirens.

"Keep going," Corey ordered.

I rolled my eyes at his drunken request. "Naw, babe. Let me pull over. We too fucked up right now," I said. I pulled over to let the police go by, but to my surprise, the cops pulled up right behind me.

"Put your seat belt on," Corey demanded, and before I could even grab mine, my door came flying open.

"Get out the car now!" one of the cops yelled.

I raised my hands up and hopped out of the car. This same cop slammed me up against the car and read me my rights while the other officer handcuffed me. I saw a man in plain clothes drag Corey out of the car. He was lying on the ground facedown.

"What the hell are you doing?" I shouted at the plain-clothes officer.

"Have you been drinking?" asked the second cop, the one who had handcuffed me.

"Blow on this!" the first officer barked at me, then shoved a Breathalyzer in my face.

As I half blew on it, I looked over at Corey, and my heart sank. One of the officers had found the drugs. The plainclothes guy began to search our car. When I was done blowing, the first officer told the second officer that I was way over the legal limit.

"What you want, man?" I asked. "I'm confused as hell!"

The plainclothes officer came out of the car, holding my driver's license. "Well, well, well, Tenosha Rivers," he said as he stood in my face. "You are under arrest for possession and manufacturing, and for driving while under the influence. . . ."

His voice trailed off, as I had blocked him out. I was in shock. Corey and I had just got busted for selling drugs. Therefore, I was right: they really had been watching us. My heart sank some more. I looked back to find Corey. They had loaded him into the police car. He was looking right at me.

"Ms. Rivers, are you not going to respond to me?" the plainclothes officer asked me.

I looked back at him with so much anger within me. Rage filled my drunken body. I slurred at the man, "Fuck you!"

"Get her in the car!" he ordered.

As they dragged me to the car behind the one Corey was in, my eyes locked with Corey's for a minute. As they threw me into the car and slammed the door behind me, I realized what was going on.

Those bitches were really taking me to jail.

Chapter 35

When I got to the jail, they took me in a different way than they did my boyfriend. They fingerprinted me, took my mug shot, and then they started my booking process. Since it was already after midnight, they told me they were going to put me in a holding cell until I could see the judge the next morning. I asked for my one phone call. After waiting almost an hour, I was finally permitted to make my call.

"Hello?" I heard a sleepy voice answer.

"Justine!" I cried out. I choked out what had happened to me.

"Where the hell is Corey at?" Her sleepy voice sounded not so sleepy anymore.

"On the other side. Justine, I won't know my bail until the morning. Will you please tell Grandma?"

I felt like a total idiot. I'd never been to jail before. Never even been caught up behind drugs in my life. I knew my grandma was going to be pissed. Another reason for her and my family not to like my guy.

Justine assured me she would be here to holla at me first thing in the morning. They took me to my cell shortly after I wrapped up my call. It had a hard bed and a toilet. They gave me a blanket but no pillow. I really had to use the bathroom, but I was scared of what was in the toilet.

I sat on the hard mattress as I debated whether or not to use the bathroom. When I finally decided to go, I squatted, not allowing my cheeks to touch the rim. I curled up in a ball once I was finished using the toilet and rocked myself to sleep.

At about nine the next morning, the bailiff came and got me. He walked me down this hall and led me into a room. When I walked in, a bald, skinny man wearing glasses was sitting behind a desk. He was looking at some papers and barely looked up at me. He set my bail at eighty thousand dollars. My mouth dropped. I was shocked and angry.

After he did that, I had to change out of my wardrobe and into a blue jumpsuit. They gave me sandals to wear and a bracelet to put around my wrist to identify me. After that, I was ready to go to my initial visit. I cried the entire time. From the moment my ass hit that stool seat in the visitors' room, tears were falling down my face. I didn't need a mirror to see that my face was red and puffy.

My mom, Drew, and Justine were all there. When I picked up the phone and saw the look on my mom's face, I burst out crying once again. Tears came rushing out of my eyes uncontrollably. My mom talked calmly to me, asking me not to cry, for about ten minutes. When I finally calmed down, my mom told me what all my charges were.

"You were driving while under the influence, you sold drugs to an undercover, they got you for possession and manufacturing, and they found marijuana seeds in the rental." My mom sounded like a robot as she repeated all the charges back to me.

By the time she finally finished, my head was spinning. I was second-guessing some of those charges and was confused. Like, what the hell did all that mean? There was no way we had that many charges! It was like those muthafuckas had made up some shit.

"What am I supposed to do, Ma?" I asked her.

For once, I wished that she would let me know every-thing was going to be okay. But it wasn't. Plus, I was worried about Corey. I talked to my mom for a minute. Then I talked to Justine. She assured me that she was going to clean out my apartment, talk to the landlord, and go talk to the manager on duty at my job as well.

"We got to try to get them to lower your bond, sis," she said to me. "Or we ain't gonna be able to get you out. We have, like, twenty-five hundred, but that's about it." That was when I heard Drew ask if we had any money put up somewhere in the house.

"You guys can go look and see. I really do think we spent every dime on that stupid-ass party."

Justine relayed the message to Drew.

A gut-wrenching feeling overcame me. I began to silently hope and pray that we did have something set aside. I explained to Justine where they could find some more cash, if we did indeed have any, but I doubted it. We talked a little bit more, and then Drew got on the phone.

"What's up, li'l bro?" I asked him.

He looked back at me with the saddest expression painted across his face. "Now is the time you are going to see how much Corey really loves you. You'll see if he's going to man up to them charges or expect you to take them," Drew said to me.

"What the hell, Drew?" I said to him.

I was already fucked up about this whole situation. My brother bringing this shit up now made me feel even worse and made me panic even more. I knew Corey. I doubted he'd have me take the charges, knowing I had four kids. Or would he expect me to take them? After all, he was on parole. This was an automatic ticket back to prison. Here I was, though, with no priors. Now my brother really had me stressing.

However, I was his girl, and I needed to step up to the plate and stay down for him, period. No matter what the outcome was. I was the one he had asked to be his better half. I was going to take that role and position seriously. I mean, this whole situation was fucked up, and taking those charges would definitely mess up my name. It was hard enough for people to get a job with even a misdemeanor on their record. Hell, an assault charge included! I had felony charges pending. Felony!

"Don't worry, sis," Drew assured me.

I could tell he could sense I had a lot on my mind at that moment. I really appreciated that all three of us siblings had such a close bond. We stayed down for each other, right or wrong.

The guard called my name to let me know I had five minutes left. It was fixing to be time for me to go back. We finished up our visit, and the guard led me to my cell.

It was a four-person cell. It had two bunk beds that sat across from each other. There was a blanket hanging on the back of each bed. There was a toilet on the far side of the cell. Around the corner from the toilet was the shower area. I was locked up with a blond chick, a mixed girl, and a fat black girl.

As soon as they opened the iron door and I walked inside the cell, they slammed the door shut behind me. *Clack-clack*. The foul odor of rotten pussy, girls on their period, and dirty asses and feet insulted my nose immediately. I couldn't even say a word, because it smelled like raw coochie so bad. It made my stomach almost turn over immediately. I just knew I was going to throw up. I didn't. I held my own.

"Yo' ass sleepin' up top," the black girl barked at me. "And you better not be stankin', either."

That last remark she made took me aback. She was telling me I better not be stinkin', but this whole damn place smelled disturbingly. She must have grown accustomed to it. I was just confused how she could fix her mouth to say such a thing, as if she couldn't smell the same shit I did.

I ain't said shit, though. I just climbed on top of the bunk and sat there, clutching my blanket to my chest. I kept thinking that the cell they had me in was nasty. The girls looked disgusting, and somebody was foul. But she wanted to tell *me* I better not be stankin? Girl, boo! The bad part about the raw stench was that you couldn't tell if it was coming from my tank or another tank.

"I'm Casey. Who are you?" the blond chick said to me.

She was lying on the bunk across from mine. She had the top one as well. She had a neat French braid coming from her head. She was very tan and was looking at a magazine.

"Tenosha Rivers," I said to her.

I was holding on to my blanket for dear life. I tried to act like I could handle this shit, but I ain't built for this shit. I was scared as hell and did not want to be here at all. I wanted to go home.

"Relax, bitch. Ain't nobody gonna fuck with yo' ass!" the black girl boomed from the bottom bunk. "What the fuck you in here for?"

On command, I recited what had happened. The black girl was terrifying. I knew immediately that she ran shit around here. I was going to do whatever was humanely possible to stay on her good side.

"You out of here, li'l mama," the mixed girl said, emerging from the shower area. Her hair had drawn up into tight curls that encircled her head like those of Shirley Temple. Almost like mine but not quite. "He gonna want you to accept them charges too."

"He on parole too? Hell, yeah, he is," the black girl said, chiming in.

The mixed girl extended her hand to me. "I'm China," she said.

I told her my name.

"I'm in here for almost the same thing. My charges ain't as long," China revealed. "My nigga had a meth lab in the basement of the house I was renting. He got caught up with it, and I was at work, at Best Buy, when the shit hit the fan. They ran all up and through my shit. Guess what? I get arrested too because it's my house. The house was in my name, and now he acting like the shit ain't his."

"I know that nigga Corey too," the black girl said, butting in, changing the subject entirely. "He a ho. Scary little punk bitch. That's some shit I'd see a ho-ass nigga like him doing. Getting his girl to take the charges 'cause he too much of a bitch to man up and do the time himself. You better not take those charges, girl. You'd be a silly, dumb-ass bitch if you did."

Chapter 36

I had been locked up for almost a month. Corey had been writing me from the other side. My sister, my mom, Bruce, and Drew were on my visitors' list. I was getting my visits on a regular twice-a-week basis. I had learned that my grandma had allowed my kids to go live with Bobbie, and now I was missing my babies more than ever.

I had also learned that some of my charges were slowly being dropped, but my bond was still high as hell. Casey had shown me how to file motions to have my bond reduced. Bruce and Justine were working on getting me a lawyer so I wouldn't have to get a court-appointed one.

I slept a lot during the day and seemed unable to keep my food down. I had quite a bit of money on my books. I was grateful for my brother and sister. They were truly looking out for me during these crazy-ass times. Majesta and my family kept money on their phones so I could call them. They kept me updated on what was going on in the streets.

On my way back from my visit with Drew one day, I passed out in the hallway and I was taken to the infirmary. The nurse didn't like the fact that I had skipped out on breakfast due to not being able to keep my food down. I explained to her that I thought that I was just too stressed, to the point that I was depressed. She thought otherwise and made me take a pregnancy test. That was when I learned that I was expecting. I felt dumb, really.

As many kids as I had, and it had never once struck me that I was carrying. I was going to have my fifth child, this one with Corey. That was when I knew I had to get the fuck up out of here.

When I got back to my cell, the guard had me and China switch places. She got extra pissed and tried to throw her weight around with the guards. They pretty much told her to calm down or go to the hole. Since I was a mommy to be, I had to sleep on a lower bunk, and she'd been there long enough to understand what the rules were in that jail. She simmered down and moved her ass around. They were also going to make sure I got plenty of juice, milk, and water throughout the day.

"You're pregnant?" Delila asked me once the excitement between China and the guards had died down.

I had learned that was the name of the black girl. Whenever I could keep my eyes open, I'd rebraid her hair, and China even had me doing hers. It helped make me extra money, and consequently, I could get calling cards and make commissary.

"Yeah," I told her.

They all congratulated me. I thanked them. Half of me was in disbelief that I was expecting, and the other part was disgusted that I had to celebrate my news, let alone learn about it, behind these suffocating walls. I wrote a kite to shoot over to my man to let him know we were expecting. I also called Majesta and Justine from the pay phone to let them know too. I hit Majesta up first.

"What's up, Ten?"

"Girl, nothing much. Just the same ole same ole. Tryin'a stay sucker free. What's good with you? What's going on out there? Your sisters still tripping with them girls in the hood?"

I let her give me the latest scoop about the latest events going down out there. Then I gave her information we were hearing in here. I always used to hear that the people in jail knew everything that was going on before those in the free world did. That was the damn truth! I knew more shit about what was going on in other people's relationships than I had when I was free. I had been totally blind to all this when I was free. Right when my fifteen minutes were about to come to an end, I broke the news to my best friend.

"I found out today that Corey and I are going to have a baby."

"You are?" I heard Majesta say. "I'll be up there tomorrow to put money on yours and big bro's books. I'll pull him out for a visit and let him know too."

"Cool, 'cause I sent him a kite. I just don't know what time they get it over there."

"Don't worry, friend. I got you ten times over."

We talked for just a little bit more, until my fifteen minutes had run out. Then I got off the phone. China was watching me from her top bunk. I lay down on my bunk and closed my eyes. I was ready to get some sleep. She wanted to talk. She called my name. I leaned my head to the side, then looked up at her.

"I just want to know one thing," she began.

"What's that?" I stared at her, wondering what off-the-wall shit she was going to say next.

"You're on your fifth kid. What if they don't let this nigga out? What if you get probation and he gets sentenced to twenty-five years? You got a felony on your record. What are you going to do?"

"You ain't gonna be able to get food stamps. Can't get HUD for a few years or help with child care. The government won't help people with drug felonies," Delila said, pitching in.

I shook my head. "I'm just going to have to maintain. That's all," I said.

The girls laughed at me. I just shrugged it off. I knew plenty of convicted felons walking around the Lene with food-stamp cards. I knew some felons who were women and had CCMS right now. I wasn't sure how long these bitches had been locked up, but I wasn't that green to the streets. If I had to wait a few years for HUD to come back up, so be it. But I was going to maintain, no matter what.

"Good luck with that, girl," Casey said.

Three weeks later, I received good news from Bruce when he and my sister pulled me out for a visit. Bruce, Justine, and Majesta had come up there to visit me and Corey on a Sunday night. Bruce was starting the visit with me and ending with Corey. Majesta was talking to Corey first. They had come to let me know that they had hired me a lawyer. They informed me that I had a court date coming up in a month and a half. I was supposed to be hearing from my attorney shortly.

"Thank you, Jesus!" I shouted loudly once Bruce delivered the good news, followed by the details.

"We gotta get you out of here. You being pregnant, that's the last place you need to be," my brother-in-law said to me.

I nodded my head in agreement.

I talked with him for a while, and then my sister got on the phone. I watched as Bruce kissed my sister and then walked out to go finish up with Corey.

"What's up, big sis?" Justine asked me.

"How are my kids?" I said, ignoring her question.

I was sincerely worried. Bobbie hardly ever accepted my calls. My mom and Justine went and picked the kids up every day, but I never knew when they had them. Karen wasn't interested in talking on the phone. Tyrese talked to me mostly. I'd spoken with Hanson twice and with Marie only once.

They'd come up to the jail a couple of times, but I had asked Justine not to bring them up here anymore. They had cried hard both times they saw me, and I couldn't take seeing them like that. I hated for them to see their mom in a damn jumpsuit and to have to look at me through a medium Plexiglas window. No hugs, no kisses, just voices and sad faces. I couldn't go home with them, and they for damn sure could not stay here with me.

"They're good," Justine said to me. She told me that they were excited that they might be getting a new brother or sister. "I spoke with Corey yesterday."

"What is he talking about?" I asked her.

"He said he was going to take his charges to trial. He's hoping that the majority of the charges will drop off for him too. He doesn't think he'll do much time at all," Justine explained.

I nodded at her. I let her know I was aware of the plan.

"He just wants you and the baby to have the proper care."

"Yeah, I know. If I get out, I don't know what I'm going to do with five kids," I said to her.

"We are going to help you, Ten. That's what family is for."

"I know," I said to her. "I'm going to need all the help I can get, Justine. I really fucked up this time."

Chapter 37

Dollie

Drew's lips felt amazing against mine. For a second, I was sucked into our own little world. I felt like I was floating on cloud nine. Like it was just us two, literally, and at that moment, nothing and nobody else mattered but us. My feet never left the ground, but my soul did. When he finally let me go, I stepped back.

"You deserve so much better," he said. He grabbed a lock of my hair with his fingers and stated," I can be that man for you if you would just give me that chance."

His arms felt the best. His eyes were filled with so much affection. The kind I had been missing in my relationship with my ex. I was soaking this entire moment in. Then a disturbing thought occurred to me right then.

"What about Corey?" I said.

I suddenly found myself in a state of confusion. I had not once thought that I should make Drew leave. I didn't want him to go, not after that kiss. But he was Corey's friend, and that creep was dating his sister. How was that going to factor in? I definitely wasn't going to be buddy-buddy with Corey and that piece of trash he was with. He wasn't welcomed in my home, either. But Drew was showing me a side to him I had never seen before. If he was trying to win me over, it was working.

"That's my boy," he said.

He gently let go of my hair and reached for my hand. Without missing a beat, I took his hand in mine. We walked over to the swing on my porch and sat down. He turned his body to face mine.

"I saw a lot of foul shit," he began. "I feel bad about not letting you in on what was going down." He shrugged his shoulders. "I was stuck between a rock and a hard place." He looked at me, his eyes pleading with mine.

A hint of anger consumed me. I was disappointed that this was ruining our moment. I thought I had gotten over the situation. I folded my arms across my chest. I leaned back, glared at him.

"A hard place and a fuckin' rock, huh?" I asked with frustration in my voice.

Drew looked taken aback.

"You motherfuckers made me look like a fool!" I said, raising my voice a little. "Do you have any idea how I felt when I found out the truth? No woman should ever have to endure that type of fuckin' treatment. I was too good to that damn punk, and that little bitch did me dirty. All of you were in on that. So what you mean, a hard place and a fuckin' rock? It's not hard to tell the damn truth!"

"If I had told you, would you have believed me?" He glanced down. "That's my sister, he was my homeboy at the time, and you're my friend. What could I do, Doll? Tell me honestly how I should have handled the position I was in."

I looked at him, and my heart immediately began to soften. Drew had come to me, alone. He had come to me with his heart on his sleeve, he had not asked me for anything, and he wasn't expecting anything in return. None of that at all. But in the past few months I had experienced one horrible train wreck that unfolded in extremely slow motion.

I took Drew's hand and began to think about what he was trying to explain. I couldn't blame him for staying out of the mix. I couldn't get mad at Drew for not wanting to tell me. Yet I still felt like him being around Corey made it look as if he was condoning the shit. I could be upset about that part. I just couldn't hold every man responsible for my ex's mistakes. Especially the ones who showed interest in me and were really good men with big hearts. I couldn't do it.

True, Drew was Tenosha's little brother. They were close, so I could see why he felt like he needed to look the other way and not speak about it. Drew was always respectful to me and nice. I had always been attracted to him in a low-key way, anyway, so why not? It was not like we were jumping the broom. Getting to know him was harmless. And I dared Corey to say something. He chose. Now I could be free to choose too.

"Do you really like me?" I asked, grilling him.

He pulled me over to him and wrapped his arms around me. He kissed my forehead. It couldn't be wrong if it felt right to be held by somebody who was showing me that he wanted me. His body language was speaking the same as mine. I was digging that.

"I've always said I wanted a woman like you," he whispered in my ear. "I'm sorry for my part in all of that. For not saying anything. For just going along with it all. Accept my apology please, Dollie. If I could take it all back, I would."

I rested my head on his chest and remembered what my aunt Audrina used to say to me. *What goes around always come back around.* I'd always given, and I'd never received. I was able to rest at night, knowing that the seeds Corey had planted would soon come back around to him in one way or another.

The man I loved the most had shunned me and humiliated me. I had had to walk with my head held high, knowing that people were clowning me behind my back. Knowing that people were looking at me like I was a stew head because of the way that little boy was treating me.

Throughout all of that, I had managed to stand up and put myself back together. I had done it for my son. I had done it for myself. I had made that effort to help myself. I had done it to continue to be about the things I believed in. I was a strong woman. I was educated. I was not going to let somebody who was lower than me bring me down any further than he had already tried to. I was better than that. Period.

Drew was a lot like me. He had chosen all the wrong girls, had tried to take care of women, and had never gotten that same treatment back. Corey was back in jail, surprisingly enough. Drew had never changed while dealing with his sister's and Corey's cases. He was steadfast. I was already cut for this man, and it was clear to me he felt the same for me too.

"I want to give you that chance. Just be with me, Drew. God will take care of the rest," I said to him.

He nodded in agreement and kissed my forehead.

If anything, God had made me a believer that everything happened for a reason. Corey and I weren't meant to be together. The truth of the matter was, he wasn't man enough for me, and God didn't like ugly. When you did ugly things to people, the outcome might be sweet, but only for a short time. That ugly you did would come back to you. But I was glad everything had happened the way it had. I was even glad about all the hurt and pain I had experienced. Because at the end of the day, you couldn't really say you had loved unless you'd been hurt before. I cozied up to Drew, and I wondered whether this was what it was supposed to feel like.

"How long, Drew?" I asked.

He looked at me and asked me what I meant. We rocked in the swing in silence for a little while. I smiled to myself and bit my lip before I gained the courage to explain what I meant.

"How long have you liked me? Why didn't you just say so?"

He shrugged his shoulders. "I have felt like this for a minute. But I always thought that you were so sprung off Corey. Felt like it was a waste of my time. Then I seen how you reacted when shit finally hit the fan. Witnessed how you weren't even contemplating going back this time. Or letting him slide. You held your ground. I knew you were done with him. In my book, you were free game."

I looked up at him, and he stared down at me. He kissed my temple once again. Held on to me even tighter.

"We're both looking for the same thing. You can't love someone and not have respect for them. We've been through the same things, different situations. I can love you, Dollie. I really can if you just give me a chance. I will not disappoint you," he said softly.

I guessed Jazzy was right, after all. Maybe I did have to go through that bullshit to get to this. All I knew was that whatever "this" was, I was sure glad to have it. Maybe good really could come from bad.

Chapter 38

Tenosha

The sheriff's car pulled up to the courthouse. The officer got out, opened the back door, and let the other two girls out before me. I glanced up at the sky when my shackled feet hit the ground.

Please, God, I prayed silently to myself. *Help me get through this. Let me go home, Father God.*

We filed into the courthouse in a single line. I was hoping that I would see my mom, my sister, or my brother. Instead, they made us use a different entrance so we wouldn't run into any civilians. We rode an elevator to the third floor. The court bailiff and his coworker ushered us into a small room.

The room was severely cold. All four walls were covered in ugly gray wallpaper. The outside of the door was red, but the back of the door was a dingy gray color. The marble floor was a pasty white color. The chains that cuffed my ankles scraped loudly against the floor. Nothing was in this room but several brown and gray chairs that were folded up against the walls. We each grabbed a chair and unfolded it so we could have a seat.

"You ladies wait here. We'll come and get you when it's your time," the bailiff said. He closed the door and locked it behind him.

As I sat on one of the cold gray chairs, I leaned my head down to rest it on my cuffed wrists. I began another round of prayers. I was so nervous, I was shaking as I awaited my fate. I wanted to get this shit over with.

The redheaded girl turned to me and asked, "Whatcha comin' to court for?"

She had brown, cat-shaped eyes. I could tell by the holes in her ears, lip, chin, and nose that she was a stoner girl. Her hair was braided back into six thick braids. She was a little on the heavy side and had several Chinese character tattoos on her arms and her neck.

I shook my head, as if to clear my jumbled mind. I was aware that there were other women with me. Up until then, my stomach was all in knots and I wasn't paying anybody else any mind.

"Trying to get my bond reduced," I murmured.

All I could think about was my kids. I wondered how Hanson was doing in school. Did Marie ever get her last hepatitis shot? I knew Tyrese was loving being with his daddy. Would Karen still remember me? This had hands down been the absolute worst four months of my life.

"What's your name?" asked a quiet voice from across the room.

I looked up to see a light-skinned, petite girl watching me curiously. She was out of the way of what little light we had in the room, but I could see that her long, curly hair flowed down her side, almost touching her thighs.

"Ten. And yours?"

The girl leaned back in the seat. Her voice was filled with that "I don't give a fuck" attitude when she said, "I'm Joslyn. My girls call me Josie. What you do? You seem like a blue-collar chick."

I sat straight up in my chair. Where did I begin? Everybody I'd talked with kept saying Corey had messed up my life. Well, at least the ones who didn't know us.

"Caught a dope case. I'm trying to get my bond reduced."

"A dope case?" the redhead asked, jumping in. "Either you are really broke or you got caught with a lot of dope if you asking for your shit to get lowered."

I sighed loudly. I looked at the two girls. They both seemed like they had been through this before. I didn't feel like repeating my story all over again. Hearing another set of opinions was not going to do anything but make my mind wander in a negative way. It was hard to stay positive in a place where there literally wasn't anything to smile about.

"I'm Myra," the redhead said, introducing herself. "I know I am going back to the pen. I ain't even sweating this shit. Give me my sentence so I can get this shit over with."

"Shit. I feel the same fuckin' way. Give me my sentence so I can get this shit behind me. The faster I get sentenced and shipped off, the sooner I'll get home to my two sons," Joslyn said, concurring.

"Y'all talkin' like y'all been through this shit before," I noted.

Both girls burst out laughing.

"I've been in and out of jail since I was sixteen. I'm twenty-eight now," Myra said, like it was really something to brag about.

"Shit. Ever since I got with the father of my children, my life been hell. Six years of having to take cases and charges for him. You know what he did to me?" Joslyn questioned.

She leaned forward and stared me dead in my eyes. The room grew silent while Myra and I waited for her to continue. Suddenly she got up and walked over to me.

"That nigga had three kids on me. I used to get my ass beat. He cheated on me constantly. I get stuck with something I didn't do, but somehow he figured out a way for me to take the rap. Now me and my sons are suffering still. When I get out, I ain't staying with his ass no more," she said.

"Damn." That was all I could say.

Those words had cut me to the core. I just found it coincidental that we were talking about this shit. To hear somebody else having to go through some bullshit was fucked up, yet refreshing at the same time. I wasn't the only one who had got it bad, who had made fucked-up decisions. I closed my eyes and immediately went back to praying.

I remained quiet, saying Hail Marys to myself. Myra and Josie began to talk among themselves, familiarizing each other with their cases. I had yet to volunteer my business to them. I hated to admit it, but I just didn't want to continue going through the judgment process with everybody. The fate of my future was in the hands of a white man. I didn't deserve to be in this shit. Now I had to deal with it.

Only thirty minutes later, which seemed like an eternity, the bailiff showed up with my attorney. They both motioned for me to follow them. We headed toward the courtroom. As we walked, my lawyer talked.

"A lot of the charges were dropped against you, but with you being pregnant, I know I can get you out, pending trial. The county is not going to want to pay for you to birth a baby. They'd rather you handle it yourself and foot the bill. Your sister and brother say that they have three thousand, so we will see how much we can get your bond reduced."

"Thank you, Jesus. Please look out for me," I pleaded out loud and in my mind.

We entered the courtroom, and to my relief, my mom, my grandma, my sister, her husband, and my brother were all there. To my surprise, some of my homegirls and homeboys from the neighborhood were there too. The support made me feel ten times better. The love was coming in all directions.

Judge Cole told us to be seated. My attorney began his spiel, requesting that my bond be lowered and that I get out from under supervision. Then, the district attorney dropped an iron on me.

"Your Honor, this young lady verbally assaulted a police officer, she was under the influence when she was arrested, and she had controlled substances in her possession. There were empty beer bottles visible to the arresting officer."

"With all due respect, Judge, this woman is pregnant, and jail is no place for her to be in right now. What's more, she's not a flight risk at all," my counsel rebutted.

Judge Cole called me to the stand. I walked over, sat down, and my attorney asked me a series of questions. I began to feel overwhelmed. Every time I thought I was going to break down and cry, I dug my nails into my cuffed hands. I held it all together. I just wanted court to be over. I answered each question to the best of my ability. Then the district attorney started in.

"Who's Corey Knight to you?"

"My fiancé," I answered.

"And what happened the night you were arrested?"

I choked back tears. I refused to cry in front of the homies. I refused to look soft in front of them all. Once again, I answered, willing myself to stay strong and remain calm.

"I honestly don't recall."

"You were that intoxicated?" he asked, with a sickened look on his face.

"What's that report say? You know if I was drunk or not," I retorted.

"So, the night you left your engagement party, were you aware that you were pregnant then?"

"No, sir. If I had known, I would not have been drinking," I assured him.

"Why do you deserve to go home and have your bond lowered?" he asked me.

"I made a mistake," I pleaded. "I need to get home to my kids, and I'm pregnant. I'm not a bad person. I just made a bad decision."

"You made several bad decisions, Ms. Rivers. Were you thinking about your kids when you guys were caught selling drugs to an informant? If you require an opinion from me, I don't think so." The D.A. took a seat, and the judge dismissed me from the bench.

The bailiff ordered everybody to rise as I took my place beside my attorney. Tears slowly trickled down my face as I begged God in my head to let the judge grant this reduction. It seemed like I was upright for the longest time. Waiting for him to decide my faith. Sweat was forming on my forehead and the bridge of my nose as I waited on his verdict. *Please let me go home, God*! I begged once more.

The judge was speaking, and I couldn't comprehend a word he was saying. He sounded awfully close to a robot moving in slow motion. All of a sudden, I felt my sister, Justice's arms around me.

"Tenosha! You're coming home!" she squealed.

Man, was my heart filled with joy. I didn't know what to do. I was flooding inside with pure relief and happiness. But even though I got to go home now, what home was that? My baby daddy had my kids. I had lost my apartment when Corey and I got arrested. And I might have to go back to prison, based on the felonies I just caught. I might be free now, but I might not be later.

Was all of this worth it? I loved Corey so much, but I guessed the grass wasn't always greener on the other side. I was carrying his baby, so now what?

Chapter 39

Dollie

Five years later . . .

"Mom, hurry, before my grandma gets here!" Drake demanded as I finished pulling the last few weeds from my garden.

I looked at my handsome little boy as he waited impatiently for me. He had his hands on his hips and was standing there with a scowl on his face. His grandma was on her way to take him for the weekend, and he was ready to go. It warmed my heart that she played a large role in his life. He couldn't have his daddy, but he had her.

I stood and headed inside, Drake on my heels. I washed my hands in the kitchen sink. "I need to check your suitcase before she arrives," I informed him as I dried my hands. I headed in the direction of his bedroom.

"I don't know why you always have to come and check my suitcase for me. I'm a big boy. I can do it all by myself," he said, pouting, as he walked behind me.

"How about you shut up before you get a big boy spanking?" I commanded.

That shut him up real quick. I walked into his very clean room. I began rummaging around in his suitcase to be certain he had packed all he needed. Right when I was zipping it up, I heard the voice of Drake's grandma as she made her way down the hall, and then I heard my husband, Drew's voice. Drake took off running in that direction.

"Grandma! Grandma!" His excitement rang throughout the house as he called out to her.

"There goes my big boy!" I heard her say.

I snatched his suitcase up off the bed once I had gotten it closed. I headed down the hallway to greet them. We stood in the hallway and chatted for a while. She filled us in on the basketball game she was taking Drake to and the hotel they were going to be staying at. He was going to have a blast with his grandma in San Antonio, and the look on his face told me he was ready to go. I also knew she had a surprise for him. She planned to take my son to SeaWorld to see Shamu.

I hugged Drake and his grandma and told my son to be on his best behavior. Then I went into the kitchen to order me and my husband some Chinese food. While I was ordering, my baby, Drew, walked them outside and saw them off. I was finishing up when he came back inside.

I loved my new life. I had never even seen this coming, but I enjoyed every minute of it. If somebody had told me eight years ago that I would be happy and in love, I would not have pictured this. I would have thought that it was for me to be happy with Corey, not Drew.

But what this man was offering me right now, at this very moment, I had never been able to imagine with my ex. God had known what he was doing when he allowed that door to close shut permanently.

Shortly after Drew and I had started dating, he moved in, and it didn't take long for Drake to like him, either. My aunt and uncle were fond of Drew as well. My uncle Justin had given him a job at the bakery. Drew and Victoria had even ended up running it together so that my uncle could open up a new barbecue shop downtown.

Once my uncle got the barbecue shop up and running the way he liked it, he was flooded with business, so he brought Drew over there. That was only because we had a barbecue at my house. When my aunt and uncle came over one time for dinner, Drew fired up the grill and then manned it, and my uncle was enthralled by his skills. Even Drew's secret sauce captivated my uncle. Drew had learned the recipe from his family and had just added some of his own elements to it. Now Drew managed the barbecue place, and my cousin managed the bakery for my uncle.

I was currently getting my bachelor's degree in criminal justice at Hardin-Simmons. I was also working as a paralegal for my boss, Jerry, at the same firm. He had just picked up a partner, whom I also loved. Her name was Roxanne Dorsi, and she mainly handled all the misdemeanor cases and the second- and third-degree felony charges when Jerry was too busy to take them. We had been bringing in enough money at the firm to have two paralegals, an office manager, and a receptionist, and I had got to train them all.

The office manager position was one that Jerry had created for me, but I had confided in him one afternoon that I really wanted to be a paralegal. I wanted to do the things that Tammy was doing for him, because I saw myself as one day being the kind of lawyer he was. He had eaten that up. He'd footed the bill for me to go to Cisco College to become a paralegal, and while I was studying full-time, he still paid me the same salary I had been making while I was in the office. Jerry had hired a new office manager, but upon hiring her, he'd made it clear that I had the final say if he wasn't around to give orders.

Tammy had gone off to law school at the University of Texas, but she always stopped by to see us whenever she was in town. She often called to get advice from Jerry and to clue him in on things that were going on in that area. I even called her from time to time to get advice on how to handle the research on some cases.

Tammy was my law big sister. She had an answer for everything, and I aspired to be as knowledgeable as she was. Jerry had trained us both so well. Now I got to step it up a notch and do the work that Tammy had performed. I wanted him to be glad that he had invested in me and my future. I was going to make my boss proud while I reached my goals at the same time. I was also preparing to work toward my master's in criminal justice, so I could become a defense attorney, but I wanted to go to Texas Tech for that when it was time.

My uncle Justin was currently looking to open up a sandwich and bakery shop in Lubbock. He was hoping that Drew and I would moved down there and Drew would take over that business as well. My husband seemed not to mind. He loved to cook, and it kept him out of trouble. He wasn't missing that street money. The business was doing so well that he was making a decent amount of money. Plus, my uncle Justin wasn't a stingy man. He didn't believe in slaving his employees. He wanted them to eat just like he did. In his mind, that was what a true boss was all about. He instilled that same mind-set in Drew every single time they talked business.

As for our relationship, lately, we hadn't had much time for each other. With my finals coming up, I was always studying. Drew had two new people at work, so he wanted to be sure they were trained properly. He was spending a lot more time at the shop. I had some very surprising news for him, and I couldn't wait to tell him.

One evening we were lounging around in the living room, watching TV and enjoying each other's company until the food arrived. We had ordered Italian food to be delivered. It had been a while since we could actually relish our time together. I had missed Drew so much and wanted to give him all the love and affection we had been missing out on due to our hectic lives.

When the food arrived, I ran to the door, grabbed the bags, and tipped the deliveryman well. Meanwhile, Drew got out plates and silverware. We devoured our meal in the living room and talked about each other's day. Once we were both done, I decided that now was the best time to let him know my secret. But something was troubling him. I could see it in his eyes. I had to learn that first before I could reveal my good news.

"What's the matter, babe?" I asked as I rubbed his neck.

"I tried to call Ten today but couldn't get in touch with her. Something ain't right."

"Well, maybe you should try calling her again. What's going on to make you feel that way? Did she say something in a prior conversation or something?" I asked, trying to sound concerned.

My ears perked up whenever he mentioned his sister's name. I no longer had hard feelings toward the girl for messing with my ex-boyfriend, but I still didn't like her. Even though I really could care less about whatever problems she was having, I gave my husband my undivided attention, so he could share his thoughts.

At the end of the day they were relatives. I was cordial to her for his sake. I want my man to be able to come to me no matter what the situation might be. Even if I didn't like it. In order for our relationship to be strong, we had to keep confronting the hard issues, even when it might seem easier to give up. We had to be each other's best friend.

"Corey has been in Abilene for two weeks, straight hanging out with this bitch. I know this man, I know he fuckin' her, and I don't like him stepping out on my sister like that."

"She doesn't know?" I wasn't surprised.

He shook his head. I could tell that this was eating at him, because Corey was his good friend and his brother-in-law. Drew had got to be Corey's best man at their courthouse wedding. I knew that Drew secretly wanted Tenosha to be with somebody else. Not with Corey. It was her life, her choice. He didn't tell her what to do, just like she didn't interfere with us.

I knew he was real close to his sister and didn't want her to experience that pain. Deep down inside, though, I could really care less. Like I had said once before, what went up had to come down. When a situation began shady, it normally ended shady. I mean, what did she expect? He had had a girlfriend when she got with him. Did she not think he would do her the way he had done me?

"Maybe they just split up for a while, baby. Have you tried talking to him about it?"

I had thrown out another scenario on purpose. I didn't want him to jump to any conclusions just yet. Maybe it was because I was optimistic like that. Drew always expected the worst but hoped for the best.

"I'm going to stay out of it. I already warned her about that man, and I had thought the nigga had changed. He's right back out here in the streets, while Tenosha is in Dallas, trying to get her life together, and she's pregnant again."

"Oh, really?"

"Yeah. He's got a family with beautiful kids to think about. That nigga too busy being on some other shit to even think twice about them. Ten deserves way better than that."

I rubbed his shoulders gently. He closed his eyes. His tense shoulders finally began to relax. I had the perfect thing that would cheer him up right now.

I took a deep breath. "Well, she ain't the only one who is expecting a baby."

He looked at me with a frustrated expression on his face. I smiled to myself. That meant he was completely lost. I was about to wipe that ugly look he was giving me clean.

"We're going to have a baby too."

I watched as his frown turned into a smile around the corners of his eyes and his lips. He looked at my belly and gave me a big hug.

"I knew there was something wrong with you. All those damn mood swings lately. How did you find out?"

I laughed out loud at his comment. "I've been knowing for a minute, but yesterday I went to the doctor and confirmed it. I am about a month along. The baby should be here next summer."

"I'm betting on a boy."

"Well, I want a girl!"

"Too bad you won't get one!" he teased me as he took me in his arms. "I was blessed with you and Drake, and now you're having my baby. I love you, Doll."

"Yes, our family will be complete." I gave him a kiss to express my feelings for him. God knew I loved him too.

When one door closed, another one always opened.

Chapter 40

Tenosha

"I'm off to work, Tenosha! I will see you in the morning," Naomi sang out as she rushed through the house, grabbing her Adidas duffel bag and keys. She hurried out of the apartment.

That was my cue to get up and watch the children. I rose up from the couch and steadied myself. My constant throbbing headache was making it difficult for me to do anything simple these days. I peered at my curly hair, which was all over the place, as I passed the mirror. I could care less how I looked right now. I just wanted to see what these badass little monsters were doing at this very moment. Karen, Marie, Tyrese, Hanson and my niece, Nestle, were at the kitchen table, doing their homework.

"Hey, Mommy!" Karen called out to me as I passed by them to check on the other kids.

I greeted them all before stepping into the hallway. The door to the room that Nestle, Marie, and Karen shared was closed, as was the door to the room that Hanson and Tyrese shared. The door to the bathroom across from their rooms was also closed. My bedroom door was shut, but the door to the little kids' room was still open. I peered inside to see my two little angels, Corey Junior and Jayci, sound asleep in the bed.

I decided to go into my bedroom. When I stepped in, I saw a thick-ass letter waiting for me from my husband. He was currently housed in Tennessee Colony, Texas, at the Coffield Unit. God had blessed us both, because my husband had ended up taking all the charges for me once he learned that they had dropped the majority of the cases. His parole had been revoked, and he had to sit out two years in the TDCJ. I called it a blessing because the outcome could have been much worse. I had been expecting our kid at the time and hadn't wanted to give birth and then do a bid afterward. While he was completing his sentence, his first child, Jayci Anne, had been born.

It had been tough, but I had made it through. I had been living in Abilene, at these apartments named Abilene North, at the time. The rent had been nothing to make, since it was income based. I'd had all five of my kids with me. Getting my older four back from Bobbie had been hell due to his messy-ass mama. He'd eventually let me have them.

I had gotten my head back on straight all the way too. Nobody could deny that. Bitches would hate 'cause I didn't get no time. They'd been mad 'cause I was riding for my honey and was carrying his first daughter. I hadn't minded the hate, though. I worked at Whataburger at night and went to school to be a dental assistant during the day. I received my certificate two months before Corey got out.

When he came home, everything was good for that first year. He had gotten a trade for welding and carpentry. He was able to land a construction job three months after he came home, with the help of one of his dad's best friends. We lived a normal but frantic life. He treated my kids like they were his own, and we took them places. Jayci was really close to her daddy, and Karen even grew close to him as well.

When I found out I was pregnant with my sixth child, I had just been offered a part-time position as a dental assistant in Plano. I was planning to go to school full-time later on to become a dentist. It was an opportunity I refused to miss out on. Plus, Corey was starting to revert to that street life. He had lost his job and was back hustling again. So in order to save our family, I made the choice for us to move. I gave Corey an ultimatum: he was either for us as a family or against us. Shit was rough. I'm not going to lie. Nigga had me regretting signing that proxy and everything. He even had me wishing I had never even married his ass in the courtroom, either. He had to show me he wanted this just as bad as I did. He chose to go to Plano.

We made our way up to Plano, but I could tell Corey wasn't happy living there. He claimed he had found another construction job. I was happy to hear that, because that construction money was good. The kicker was if he took the position, it meant that he had to go back West to work in Abilene, Odessa, and Midland. My gut instinct said hell no. I pushed past that and decided to let him go.

My three oldest kids wanted to live with their dad in Abilene because they missed their old friends. So I allowed Hanson, Marie, and Tyrese to go live with Corey. But Karen, being a mommy's girl, stayed with me and Jayci.

When I was seven months pregnant, my sister called me one night to drop some dreadful news on me. My so-called working husband had been arrested in Abilene for a robbery and gun charge. So, there I was, getting my two youngest kids together and heading out to Abilene in the middle of the night.

When I reached Abilene, I left my kids at my grandma's house, then headed for the jail. When I got to the jail, I found Drew and my brother-in-law, Bruce, in the foyer with a bail bondsman.

"What the hell happened?" I asked them.

"What are you doing here, Tenosha?" Bruce asked me.

"I'm his wife. What you mean, what the hell am I doing here, Bruce? What the hell is going on?"

Something wasn't right. I could tell by the looks on their faces that something really fucked up was going on. Luckily for them, the bail bondsman disappeared and then reappeared with a dark-skinned, ugly-ass girl with a bad hair weave on her head. I mean, this ho's head was so busted, you could see the tracks rising from her head where the glue was supposed to be at. Drew and Bruce could not look at me after she came out, talking loudly, behind the bail bondsman. My heart sank in my chest right then. I instantly knew that my nigga was dealing with this trash in some type of way.

"We can't let him out. There is no bond. I was able to get Jolleen out, but not Corey," the bail bondsman reported.

My brother and my brother-in-law were trying to play it off so it wouldn't look as if the man was speaking to them. Kind of hard to pull that off when the jail was practically empty and only five people were standing in the foyer. If looks could kill, those two would be dead right now. My muthafuckin' blood was boiling right now.

"What's going on with my husband, sir?" I asked the bondsman.

The guy looked at me skeptically. He glanced over at the ugly burnt duck before answering me. Or attempting to, anyway. The girl gazed at me, with her big-ass duck lips puckered up at yours truly. I watched in dismay as this bitch had the audacity to smirk at me. *What the fuck?*

Drew grabbed me by my arm and tried to pull me out the door of the jailhouse. I wasn't having it, though. I had questions, and I wanted them responded to now, damn it! Everybody was starting to act like the cat had got their tongue. I decided to repeat myself, louder.

"I'm Tenosha Knight," I said, digging into my purse for my driver's license. Once I got it, I gave it to the bondsman. "What's going on with my husband, please, sir?"

The bondsman acted as if he was going to speak, but the duck started in first.

"You should have stayed your lazy ass in Fort Worth until you had that baby. Hell, everybody know you just got pregnant to try to trap Corey with your skank ass."

My mouth dropped. Seriously, this ho felt like it was okay to talk to me like that? *Me?* I was his wife; she was just a side bitch. A clucker-lookin'-ass side bitch. I had never felt the way I did standing in this situation as I did tonight. My mind was going a mile an hour, and my heart was bleeding. He had traded in our family for 910 South Twenty-Seventh. I hoped it was worth it.

My brother intervened in the situation, while Bruce and the girl went at it, trading verbal insults with one another. Drew led me outside and back to my car. He needed me to drive him home. That moment was when my suspicions were confirmed. I learned that my fucked-up husband had been cheating on me with this Jolleen girl.

"How long, Drew? You're my fuckin' brother, and you knew about this bitch? I'm your sister. I'd never let a bitch dog you out!"

Drew stared at me like a deer in headlights. I didn't give a fuck. I let him have it.

"How dare you not call me and give me the heads-up and shit. Blood is supposed to be thicker than water."

"Ten, I thought y'all split up. Why you think every time we talked, I asked if you had heard from him? I was under the impression that you two had split up," he explained to me.

I could tell by the way my brother sounded that he had had no idea that everything was okay between me and Corey. Corey had made it sound like I was tripping and we had split up. He had come up with this long, drawn-out story about how I had put him out of the house for coming in drunk too many times. Hearing this bullshit fucked me up. I cried the whole way to Drew's house. I even sat in my bro's driveway for a good hour, letting the tears run freely until I couldn't cry anymore. I pulled myself together and drove off.

That night, I stayed at my grandma's house. I was too dead beat to steer myself back up that highway. Before I could call it a night, I wrote my husband a long-ass letter explaining to him why I wanted a divorce. I told him that he didn't do people who cared about him the way he had done me. I even told him about how this ho had smirked at me in my face.

I had known going into this marriage with him that no matter what, I was going to have his back. Till death did us part, I was going to be with him. But now the trust had been broken, and my heart hurt from the lies he had told—all the times he had claimed he was working but was really getting into trouble in Abilene. Now I hated to admit it—God knows, I hated this to the core—but I now knew how it felt to be played like a damn fool. I got to tell you, that pain was crazy insane. Love hurt like hell. Could make you so damn blind and stupid. One thing I had done that no other bitch could achieve was become his wife. I had his last name, which meant that he was still mine, and nobody else could have him. I had the ring, the kids, and the right to claim him.

Corey Junior was born not long after. Naomi moved in with me once little man turned four months so she could get back on her feet. Before, I had just let her crash when she needed a place to stay. She was my sister-in-law, so

I looked out for her as if she was my very own. We both needed the help, which meant we could help one another. She was working at a twenty-four-hour movie theater in downtown Arlington, so I watched the kids at night, and she had them during the day, while I handled business. They loved their aunt Naomi. My sister, Justine, had taken my three oldest kids, and she came down with them often to see me and to visit her nieces and nephew.

Last weekend, when my sister visited, we had taken the kids to see the Ripley's Believe It or Not! Museum. We had gone to Jack in the Box to eat afterward, and Naomi and Nestle had met up with us. Justine wasn't too fond of Corey's sister. She was cordial, though, out of respect for me.

"You got a letter from my brother today." Naomi placed the letter in my hands and excused herself to go the bathroom. She took Karen and Marie with her.

Justine wrinkled her nose at me.

"Don't start, sis," I warned her.

"She just overdoes the shit. Does she need to announce out loud in front of everybody that you got a letter from her brother?" My sister scowled. I just brushed it off and tucked the letter safely in my purse. I needed to study it in peace, without any extra voices around me.

I was pretty sure my husband was pissed off. He hadn't gotten a visit in two weeks. I vowed to read the letter the first chance I got when I arrived home. When everybody was sleeping and the house was not stirring.

"I just see all the shit you are going through, and I wonder if this is worth it. Who is to say that Corey is going to change when he gets out? I just don't see why you can't see what his sorry ass is doing."

"We're married. I can't turn my back on him now."

"He turned his back on you. And that bitch Jolleen is still wandering around Abilene, talking about how she is his girl and shit, with her ugly ass."

I cringed at the sound of that ho's name. I had to admit, that part stung my heart like a bitch. Why should I give up on our family? All because a no-morals-having bitch wanted to ruin my happy home?

"He still writes her too," Justine said matter-of-factly.

"How do you know?" I said, interrogating her.

"Bruce told me. We didn't say nothing, because we knew you aspired to stay with him. However, it's not you. It's him. I just don't want him to damage you, that's all."

"He won't, sister."

"He better not," she stated with a threatening tone.

Even though nobody knew it, his ass already had hurt me to the core. I was just trying to deal with it by myself, so nobody knew how I really and truly felt. I was feeling trapped. I felt like I had married somebody phony, but he had chosen me to be his wife. He didn't want this marriage to end. His letters said it a million times. How much he loved me like a fat kid loved cake. That he loved me more than every letter and every word in the entire universe could express.

I was going to ride it out with him. Crazy-ass thing for me to say, since I could honestly admit, I knew how Dollie felt. However, I wasn't going to admit that shit out loud or nothing. I wasn't going to go woman up and apologize to Dollie. I felt like what I had endured was payback enough. I hadn't understood then why she was so upset when she found out about us, but I truly understood it now.

Damn. Now, ain't that a bitch?